For the
Rave
at Ky...
Best wishes!

Sanctuary
For Love

Karen Passey

Karen Passey

Sanctuary For Love

Cover design by Lee Ching / Under Cover Designs

DEDICATION

This book is dedicated to Carl

MORE BOOKS BY KAREN PASSEY

In Your Own Time
Contract For Love
When Two Worlds Collide

Sanctuary For Love

Karen Passey

CHAPTER 1

"I'm afraid that it is the only offer, Caroline, and I'd strongly advise you to take it". Sydney Devine, the small, ageless, sallow-faced accountant was trying to be firm without sounding officious. He removed his spectacles and carefully wiped the lenses on the neatly folded handkerchief he drew from his shiny pin-striped trouser pocket.

He inclined his head to one side and watched her with a thoughtful, narrow gaze. It had been hard enough for him to convince her that her father had left her a business that bordered on near-bankruptcy and the only possible solution to her financial problems was to sell.

Caroline swallowed hard, too charged with emotion to reply. She gripped firmly on the wrought iron gate that led from the garden to the complex of modern, low buildings with the network of fencing runs. Beyond the kennels lay acres of fields converging on scrub then woodland which encompassed the domain of the Franklin Animal Sanctuary and Boarding Kennels. The tears were trickling down her pale cheeks as she finally choked a response.

"I can't….I can't let it go for…." she couldn't continue.

"I don't imagine there'll be a much better offer," Mr Devine was quick to jump in.

"It isn't even the money, although it's a paltry amount he's offering. No!" She shook her head. "It's more than that, Mr Devine. This was my father's dream. If I sell up, I'm letting him down. He would never have been defeated like this." She sobbed uncontrollably, remembering a June evening two years earlier when her father had stood just where Mr Devine was now, with his arm around her shoulders, her father had gestured to the Sanctuary.

"One day Cal, this will all be yours", he had promised.

At five feet five in flat shoes, she still had to stand on tip toe to kiss her father. In every way he was tall in his daughter's eyes. A proud, honourable man, a former officer in the Royal Navy, William Franklin had carried three precepts through his life - love with honour, honour with love and work hard at both. He was a man highly respected and admired wherever he went and his early retirement from naval life had been much regretted by his superiors.

"That will be years away, Dad", she had turned her head to look into the cool blue of his eyes that were beginning now, in his fiftieth year, to show traces of tiredness. "I've so many plans to fulfil before I come home to roost."

"I know, my dear girl – I don't ever want to deny you your freedom – your wings must have their flight. I've had mine. No, you just come home when you're ready."

But life hadn't quite worked out how she had anticipated and she had been far from ready to return to England when the urgent call had come just two years later.

Her long, blonde hair strayed carelessly in the wind, blowing across her face, masking the flood of tears as she gave full rein to her emotions. There was no arm of reassurance around her now, only the cold emptiness of reality to be faced as the full extent of her loss was brought home to her, looking across at the charred remains that had once been The Cattery.

"You'll have to make a fairly quick decision", Sydney Devine interrupted her thoughts.

"What alternatives are there, Mr Devine?" Caroline, gathering control of her emotions, blew her nose unceremoniously.

"None, as I see it. Mr Sinclair's offer is likely to be the only one. The interest on the debt increases daily, as I'm sure you must be aware. You are in no position to be choosey about the purchaser, Miss Franklin."

"I suppose I could resign myself to selling, but – Alexander Sinclair – it's the last bitter blow to be dealt me in the whole sequence of disastrous events", she replied gloomily. "My, how he'll gloat!"

"You are acquainted then?" the accountant seemed surprised.

Caroline had no intention of elaborating to this mincing little man whose main concern seemed to be tidying up loose ends, settling things and closing accounts.

It seemed that the sale of the Sanctuary and Kennels would have to go ahead and Caroline would have to build a new life for herself. She cursed the fact that Alexander Sinclair appeared to be at the forefront when anything went wrong for her.

Lying in the darkness that night, she was ready to

admit that if she had never gone away to work abroad after she had qualified at Cambridge, then the whole disaster might never have happened. It had been her intention, her dream, to buy herself into the Veterinary practice in Broadway, a few miles away.

Tom Barron, the senior partner could not go on forever and he had hinted on more than one occasion that when he retired, Caroline would be a considerable asset to the partnership. She and her parents had become very friendly with Tom since establishing the Sanctuary and by the time she would finish training at Vet School, Tom would be due to retire. There seemed little doubt on either side that she would buy her way into the Practice. But there were always variables.

Hugh Morrison was one such variable.

Partway through her course Caroline took an extra year out to do an added degree in the Economics of Agriculture. It meant Tom Barron had finished work a year ahead of Caroline's qualifying. Hugh, Tom's partner, promised to keep the place open for her, but later welched on his promise when his old acquaintance, Alexander Sinclair, with whom he had been at Vet School in Edinburgh, twisted his arm to let him buy the partnership.

Caroline had choked with fury that summer.

"The only way you'll be part of this Practice, Cal, is if you marry me", Hugh had vowed.

It was a compromise she refused to accept. But there was another, stronger reason for refusing Hugh's proposal – and that was his new partner, Alexander Sinclair!

Instead, Caroline had acquired a scholarship to study dairying in Israel. A year later she had taken up the offer of an expedition to the little islands in the Artic to study avian influenza in the wild bird population there. Just after her father had made the promise about the Sanctuary, Caroline flew to Zambia to work with Save the Rhino Trust. Then she went on to Denmark to work on a pig farm. It was not work that was calculated to get her the best entry prospects into a mixed practice in the Cotswolds, but she had long since given up on that idea. Her firm intention after another couple of years of experience abroad had been to establish herself with her father at the Sanctuary and eventually set up her own practice, based at the Sanctuary.

In the longer term, she had dreams of extending the kennels, opening a riding school and later, perhaps gaining a licence to run quarantine kennels. The dreams were endless.

But dreams are not for the faint-hearted and when they are shattered beyond repair, only a dedicated optimist can have the vision to continue.

Caroline slept little that night, trying to place some perspectives for the future on her now shattered life. Very early the next morning found her leaning on the five-bar gate that led to the kennels.

"It was a high price to pay", her mother cried, touching Caroline's shoulder.

Caroline had not heard the footsteps on the gravel behind her.

"We must try to carry on, Mum, Dad would have wanted that. Never be defeated." Caroline choked at her own words, slipped her arm comfortingly around her mother, and for minutes they stood together in their mutual sorrow.

"We've got an even greater reason to make a

success of it now", she attempted for her mother's sake, to sound convincing.

"But what about the offer...? Mr Devine said...." Her mother looked at her anxiously.

"I know exactly what Mr Devine said, Mum, but I'm not dad's daughter for nothing. I've gone too far to give in so easily."

"But we'll never manage to..."

"Mother, trust me, please", Caroline begged, slipping her arm through her mother's. "Let's take a walk over to the woods, I want to talk to you." She called to the Golden Retriever, "Whistler, come girl, we're going on an all-woman walkabout."

Mrs Franklin looked anxiously over her shoulder. "Mr Sinclair promised to look in and check the cats over", she said distractedly.

"Mother – I'm the Vet around here now – we don't need Sinclair – we don't need anyone, but we especially don't need him! If it hadn't been for Dad relying on other people none of this might have happened". Caroline was defiant in her anger.

"We can't be sure it was Oliver's fault, dear."

At times Caroline was exasperated by her mother's magnanimity.

"Really, mother, the Fire people were practically a hundred per cent certain it was a cigarette end that caused the fire. In any case, Oliver Cory was the only one of the staff who smoked – and if it wasn't him, then where is he now? Why has he not reappeared for work? He never even turned up to Dad's funeral!" Her face flushed with passion as her anger raced on like a torrent. "If I ever meet him, I'll..."

"No dear", her mother interjected, Vengeance is mine, saith the Lord. Besides he'll have had punishment enough already. He must know if he caused the fire that he was responsible for your father's death. That will surely be on his conscience for the rest of his life."

"And what about your life?" Caroline asked bluntly.

"Mine, Cal dear, will just …" she choked on her words, then continued, "mine will just have to go on without your father."

Caroline stole a glance at her mother. Such a small, frail woman, tired and empty now, as if her whole health and well-being had been drained out of her. She was trying to be strong and the effort was painful for Caroline to observe.

As they walked, Caroline told her mother of her plans to re-build the Cattery.

"Work is the best medicine to overcome disaster and disappointment. We have to survive. But what has puzzled me more than anything is why … why would Oliver Cory do such a stupid thing? Do you think it could have been done deliberately, Mum?"

"Oh, Cal, that's a terrible suggestion!" her mother quickly opposed such a thought.

"I'm sorry, I have an awful feeling that something is dreadfully wrong somewhere. Oliver Cory ought to have re-appeared, even more so if it had been an accident, if only to defend himself."

Her mother shook her head, unwilling or unable, to dwell on her husband's horrific death any longer, and also distracted by a rider on horseback coming towards them across the scrubland from the woods.

"Who on earth is that out at this time of the morning?"

"More to the point, what are they doing on our

land?" Caroline fumed, for she could already see the rider quite clearly and needed no second look to recognise Alexander Sinclair.

She began to formulate angry questions as he slowly reined in his huge black stallion beside them. Caroline felt quite intimidated by the disparity in height now between them.

Sinclair dismounted and greeted them both warmly.

"Good morning ladies, I was riding over to see your cats."

Caroline was quick to spurn him.

"For a start, Mr Sinclair, the entrance to the Cattery is not across private land, it is from the main Broadway Road. For a second thing, it may have escaped your notice but we no longer require your services. I shall be attending to all the animals in future." She felt she had scored as she observed him stiffen slightly and his mouth quirked as he replied with a wry smile.

"Your father gave me unprecedented right of way, Miss Franklin. Of course, nothing was written down formally, it was a gentlemen's agreement". There was a note of derision in his voice.

"My father is not here now", she cut in quickly trying to put an icy quality into her voice as she could visualise her generous-natured father giving carte-blanche to this chauvinistic male who so far had caused her some considerable problems in life.

"I'm well aware of that – I was at the funeral, you may recall", he declared tightly.

"Well, you needn't be calling again, anyway, Mr Sinclair", she said, tossing her long blonde hair in an angry gesture.

"That remains to be seen for I certainly don't

intend to have my movements dictated by you. There's also the matter of my offer in with your Mr Devine…"

"And weren't you quick to make it, Mr Sinclair", Caroline flung at him furiously, reddening as her temper rose at his sheer arrogance.

"Where animals are concerned, Miss Franklin", he countered, laying heavy emphasis on her surname, "I move very, very quickly. Animals are my first concern. In any case, your father was well aware of my offer, long before this tragedy occurred".

"Just what do you mean?" she flashed angrily.

"You are obviously not well-informed", he amended with a cruel frankness.

"Are you telling me you offered to buy out my father?"

He watched her closely with a thoughtful, narrow gaze, his grey eyes burning into her. Slowly, calculatingly he responded, measuring his words in deference to her mother.

"Your father and I were friends. You may have excellent Veterinary qualifications, Miss Franklin, but you have none of your father's congeniality or civility".

He turned apologetically to Mrs Franklin, smiled tentatively, ignoring Caroline.

"This must be very painful for you. When your husband found he was running into financial difficulties, you know we discussed, as friends, how the situation could be resolved. We talked of my buying the whole Franklin Sanctuary. There was one condition to my original offer that he insisted upon. My financial offer remains exactly the same as it was before the fire, but the condition he exacted from me does not. I am, as you know, deeply sorry about the tragedy".

He touched her mother affectionately on the shoulder. "I'll call and see you soon."

As he made to mount his stallion he said in a low voice to Caroline, "For God's sake try and learn to be more civil, if only for your poor mother's sake".

Before she could answer he rode off in the direction he had come from.

Her mother was quietly sobbing. She had said nothing but she knew everything and it was clear that little of what she knew had been told to Caroline.

It was no consolation to Caroline that Sinclair had been a friend to her father. She had loved her father deeply but there were things he could not have known about Alexander Sinclair. If he had been aware of how badly Sinclair had treated Caroline, especially at Ledbury, he would never have entertained him as a friend.

No, certainly, Caroline felt sure her father would never have encouraged a man as chauvinistic as Alexander Sinclair, a man who believed that women Vets were only capable of looking after cats and dogs. His words to her at Ledbury, some four years earlier, still stung her to the quick. She was furious. He had left her mother in tears, probably not deliberately, to give him his due, but he had made Caroline feel a complete outsider. It was as if there had been some collusion, some scheme, about which she knew nothing. And furthermore, what was the condition which her father had exacted? Mr Devine had mentioned none of this.

Clearly it would be insensitive to question her mother now, but she must go to Mr Devine and find out what lay behind Sinclair's offer. In fact, she recalled how only the day before, Mr Devine had tried to urge her to make a quick decision.

As Caroline slipped her arm around her mother and they quietly walked back to the house with Whistler, the retriever, sympathetically trailing alongside, she resolved to say nothing more about the conversation with Sinclair. After breakfast she would attend to all the cats and give them a thorough health check. She would have to organise the kennel maids into activity and arrange to see Mr Devine as quickly as possible. Her sleepless night had yielded one or two possibilities as routes out of their problem without having to consider any wretched offer from Alexander Sinclair.

They stopped off at the hen house and gathered some newly-laid eggs to cook for their breakfast.

"It's just not economical, is it?" she eyed her mother who already looked weary enough before the day had half begun.

"This was your father's idea, not mine", she replied, brushing grey hairs distractedly from her face.

"It wouldn't be a weakness to give up the hens, mother – we simply can't make that side of it pay. The foxes probably do better out of it than the Sanctuary".

"I can't kill them – it defeats the object of the Sanctuary. They've already been rejected once by the poultry farm – that's how we came by them in the first place. After a year when they've practically worn the poor creatures out on the battery range, they sell them off for a pittance. Your father did think it was an act of charity more than an economical venture". Her mother's voice had a sob in it still.

"Of course we won't kill them off", Caroline agreed. "I'd never agree to that. No, I think we can ask Alice over in Stanton. She's got free range hens – she'll probably be glad of an extra thirty layers".

"If you say so dear".

They reached the house and went straight to the kitchen. Her mother absentmindedly started to lay the table for three.

"It's not just a question of economics, mother. It's also a matter of labour. Without Dad we'll have to reorganise the workloads".

"What about Oliver Cory?" Mrs Franklin queried.

Caroline cracked the eggs into the pan and continued without looking at her mother.

"I'd prefer to have an extra kennel maid, get rid of the hens and take it from there. We'll need some domestic help for the house too", she added confidently. "I lay awake half the night trying to get things into some kind of perspective. First thing is to talk to the accountant and see what provision Dad made for catastrophes like this – what contingency money there is and so on. The Cattery must be re-built", she raced on, oblivious to her mother, "we can't salvage much of it. The cats can't be housed for long in those temporary sheds."

Her mother had sat down, a weary expression on her face.

"I don't understand all this economics and contingency business, Cal your father handled all of that. I was just his…." she broke down again. Caroline took her mother's hands in hers. She had forgotten her earlier resolve to say as little as possible while her mother was still so agitated. In her anxiety to get out of the mess they were in, she had raced away keenly to find a solution to avoid taking Sinclair's offer.

"I know that you were everything to Dad", she softened her voice. "You just leave the business side to me. But I'm going to need you. You've been running the place for so long that it's second nature to you. I may be a qualified Vet, Mum, but day-to-day running is not like a text book! I shall need all the help you can give me". She kissed her mother lightly on the cheek. "Now, let's eat these eggs before they spoil and then you can tell me how you used to plan the day – what our next move is".

"Yes dear", her mother replied meekly.

Caroline knew enough of her mother, however, to realise that under the gentleness and tenderness she was a very capable organiser, despite her protestations to the contrary.

"This afternoon I have an appointment with a Mr Avery Briggs in the Vet practice in Cheltenham", she told her mother. "How would you like to drive over with me? We can leave the two kennel girls in charge for the afternoon, I'm sure".

"But you mustn't go and work for him, Cal – he's ….oh, you know, the sort of things they say about him and the women at the …"

Caroline quickly interrupted her mother.

"You simply must trust my judgment on these things, mother. In any case, he's probably not half as bad as the picture people paint. Gossip gets quite exaggerated. I'll be able to handle him", she added confidently. "At least it will be different from having to defend my professional position as a Vet, which I've had to continually do with the Barron Practice at

Broadway, and most particularly with Sinclair".

It had been easy to avoid Sinclair whenever she had come home to the Sanctuary over the last two or three years. During her short stays she would automatically take over the responsibility for any animals. On the odd occasions Hugh Morrison had called at the Sanctuary, more to pester her than to administer treatment to the animals.

She felt an overwhelming resentment towards Sinclair, not least because she felt her place at the Broadway practice had been usurped by the aggressive Scot. And she was hostile towards Hugh because of his deviousness in letting Sinclair have the partnership. Even the years that had elapsed had not at all softened her displeasure. It was aggravated by Hugh's insipid attitude towards her. Despite her protestations and refusals he seemed confident that it was only a matter of time before she would settle to become his wife. She seemed unable to make him realise, short of being downright rude, that she was refusing him. What to Caroline was worse, was the fact that Hugh had quite obvious designs not so much on her, but on the obtaining of the Sanctuary and all the Franklin acres!

Later that afternoon, after a very satisfactory meeting with Avery Briggs, she took her mother into a small tea room on the fringe of Cheltenham. She tried to put all the money worries out of the way for an hour while she attempted, with very little success, to cheer up her mother, despite the fact that she had such reassuring news about being offered a post with Mr Briggs.

As they were leaving the tea room, she was a little more than dismayed to find herself unable to avoid virtually bumping into Julia Morrison. Hugh's sister was just the sort of female Caroline couldn't stand, always immaculately groomed, expensively so too, elegant and poised, but to Caroline's mind, vacuous and empty-headed. Times out of number she had referred to Caroline as 'my little future sister-in-law'.

The size had precious little to do with Caroline's stature, since she had never felt inadequate at five feet five in her stockinged feet. Julia seemed to tower above her physically and always gave the impression that Hugh was being extremely magnanimous in offering to marry Caroline. Not having particularly much of a brain herself, Julia was incapable of understanding why some women chose to become academically qualified and follow a once-male preserve.

"How on earth you cope with that mucky farm work beats me", Julia had once attempted to brush off an indignant remark from Caroline. Fortunately Caroline had restrained herself from the obvious remark that it would appear that any kind of work would probably beat Julia!

"Caroline, darling, how delightful to see you – Alex and I were only just talking about you. "He's parking the car", she added smugly. Not in the least bit impressed at being talked about by Alex Sinclair, and more than anxious to go before he arrived, Caroline attempted to brush off the conversation with a polite, "We're in rather a hurry, Julia".

Unfortunately, Julia, insensitive as ever, immediately engaged Mrs Franklin in unhappy clichés of insincerity regarding the recent loss of "your dear husband". Caroline was sickened as she watched her poor mother's wretched face trying to bravely hold back the tears.

Julia quickly switched to her favourite topic.

"Hugh's positively dejected since you've turned down his offer, darling", she simpered.

"What offer?" Caroline knew she should have kept quiet.

"Why, for the Sanctuary, of course", Julia replied, oblivious to the anger mounting in Caroline. "It would be best all round, don't you think so, Mrs Franklin? After all the marriage is only a formality, isn't it?"

How could she be so stupid? Caroline was in a state of semi-shock, unable to find words to counter Julia's crass manner.

Alexander Sinclair, for once, saved Caroline from committing an act of violence. He must have heard Julia's whining voice and her comments as he approached, and he immediately took hold of the situation.

"Mrs Franklin – good afternoon. Julia, do go inside and find us a table, will you? I need to talk Vet talk to Mrs Franklin".

She complied in an instant, flashing an insipid grin at Caroline.

But Caroline was still peeved with Sinclair. She was in charge of the Sanctuary now, as well he knew. Why should she have need to talk about the Sanctuary anyway?

"My apologies for Julia, Mrs Franklin", he was saying, "she can be quite insensitive at times – but she intends no harm, I'm sure. Would you care to join us for tea?"

"We've taken ours, thank you just the same",

Caroline jumped in quickly, "and we're in rather a hurry, if you don't mind". She slipped her arm through her mother's and started to gently steer her away. "We've a Sanctuary to run", she added, immediately regretting her sharp rejoinder, for it gave him an added opportunity to insinuate himself further.

"You could consider my offer, Caroline", he said, a wry smile creasing his face.

"Don't push us Mr Sinclair", she said stiffly, giving nothing away.

Glad to be able to get away from him and his arrogant male dominance, Caroline couldn't help wondering what offer Hugh had made, and more to the point, why Mr Devine had not mentioned it.
Even more to the point, was Hugh aware that his partner, Alexander Sinclair had made an offer?

No matter how much she tossed these thoughts about in her mind, Caroline would have to wait until she saw Mr Devine next day. It occurred to her also that despite the fact that he told Julia he wanted to talk "Vet talk" to her mother, Sinclair had not in fact done so. She wondered what he had intended to say and how much her own angry interjections had deterred him from discussing what he had intended to. Perhaps it had just been a ploy to get rid of Julia?

Her mother was very subdued by the whole incident and not forthcoming at all. It was just as well, Caroline reflected, for her mother looked very tired. As she drove slowly back the twenty miles or so to the Sanctuary, Caroline was relieved to see her mother nod off so readily with the hum of the engine and the gentle warmth of the afternoon sun in the car.

CHAPTER 2

Caroline wasted no time in getting a local builder in to re-build the burnt-out Cattery. Having got clearance from the Insurance Company she knew that she would have an interminable wait for the money, but in the meantime they had said she could go ahead. The cats would be re-housed within two weeks. Unfortunately, all the other damaged storage sheds and the wooden garages would have to wait.

She had a job for herself lined up with Avery Briggs and had arranged with one of the kennel maids who had a sister keen to work for them.

Three days later she was hosing out the kennels when she realised Alexander Sinclair was leaning on the post at the far end of the dog run. She nodded indifferently. Most of her fury was being tamed now because she felt more sure of herself and the Sanctuary – although she still had to meet that afternoon with Mr Devine and put her cards on the table.

"Glad to see you're keeping up the good work on my proposed investment".

Her disinclination to conversation did not deter him. She gave him a steely, impersonal stare.

"My concern is for the animals, not investments", Caroline decided not to enlighten him as to her plans.

"That's precisely how Hugh said you'd react", he commented dryly, a smirk on his face.

Caroline turned, reddening with anger, half inclined to set the hosepipe on him and his arrogance.

"I'd be grateful if you'd stop discussing me with the Morrisons – it does seem to be becoming a habit with you. This Sanctuary has obviously taken up too much of your expensive time – and the emphasis, Mr Sinclair, is on the expense!"

"What exactly are you referring to?" he demanded, moving over towards her determinedly.

She stood her ground and aimed the hosepipe directly in front of herself defensively.

"My father appears to have paid an inordinate amount of money to your Practice in the last few years, which seems to have given him a considerable lift on the road to near-bankruptcy!"

Hugh had been paying a weekly call to the Sanctuary and charging her father heavily. Her father had run short of money.

"He would have paid for a veterinary service, Miss Franklin", Sinclair said quickly with acid denunciation, rising to her accusation.

She looked at him in exasperation.

"I think you've missed my point, Mr Sinclair", she retorted sharply.

"Oh no", his eyes narrowed, "I think we understand each other quite clearly. However, I maintain that from an economical point of view labour comes cheaply hereabouts, professional advice and expertise does not! And whilst we are quibbling about cost, what sort of value do you put on yourself? It seems to me that a kennel maid is paid the sort of rates to clean out the kennels – it's all down to division of labour and all that! Good morning!"

He finished sharply and stomped back to his car across the gravel before she had had a chance to reply, leaving her fuming. It also occurred to her later that she had no idea why he had come in the first place.

Every time she met Alexander Sinclair he had humiliated her with his superior attitude, always had the last word, and always left her smarting against the sting of his final retort.

This time he was right, of course. A kennel maid should have cleaned out the dog runs, but Caroline had given the girl her permission to be at a wedding in Evesham and the second girl was down with a virus. It all added up to inconvenience. Caroline felt put out by Sinclair's ability to appear at all the wrong moments, misconstrue a situation and leave with a 'score' against her.

She despised his male chauvinism, his readiness to discount the female veterinary surgeon as someone capable only of dealing with domestic pets. She would never forgive him his attitude and nothing would alter her loathing and disgust of him. Some years previously, she had spent one of her vacations working on a dairy farm near Ledbury.

She had deliberately not chosen to spend the holidays at the Sanctuary, because she was trying to gain as wide an experience as possible and besides, it would have been all too easy to simply help out at home. Instead it required a more rigid self-discipline to fall in with the rigours of early morning milking and dawn risings on someone else's property.

Jordan's Farm, near Ledbury had a sophisticated

modern dairy and arable land of around four hundred acres. Ron Jordan, a burly, rugged man with a face that looked as if it had been worn into submission by a long succession of hard winters and dry summers, was no philanthropic dairyman.

He was more than willing to accept a 'green' undergraduate at a labourer's rates and expect professional expertise for half the price. What is more, he accepted with alacrity the female of the species since it gave him ample opportunity to exert his own brand of rural male chauvinism, which she unhappily encountered one afternoon when she told him she suspected mastitis in his cows, something he strongly refuted.

"Well, something is wrong, and I suggest you call in the veterinary surgeon to investigate", Caroline tossed at him.

"You're supposed to know these things – that's what I'm a-payin' you for!" he retorted, repeating his earlier reason for employing her.

"I can't administer antibiotics, Mr Jordan", she said, her voice rising with. "I'm not fully qualified yet", she unwillingly hastened to add.

He searched her face, his eyes squinting. "You sure, now? I don't want the vet 'ere costing me if it ain't necessary". His utter stupidity and avarice stunned her.

"I'm sure you'll be justified in calling in your vet", she pronounced firmly.

It had occurred to her that he knew he had mastitis in his herd and was only trying to find a scapegoat in her. She had already been told by one of the cowmen that he had recently sacked one of them and taken on Caroline for the three summer months at half the man's pay. It was a false economy, obviously, for now he would pay heavily in vet's bills.

"Call yourself a Vet?" Alexander Sinclair had scoffed at her the very first time they met.

When finally he had arrived and after spending hours scrutinising the whole herd and injecting where necessary, Sinclair had upbraided Caroline for not recognising the signs of mastitis before. He had stood in front of her, blocking the alley in the milk parlour, his eyes running over her scornfully.

"I think I can hardly be blamed…" she started. His cruel mouth turned down at the corners and she felt herself being 'carpeted'. Physically so imposing, his broad shoulders and expansive chest tapering down to an athletic waist, he intimidated her by his presence, but overpowered her with his arrogance and refusal to listen to her.

"Don't be so adolescent Miss… whatever your name is. These may only be cattle, but they do feel – and mastitis is damned painful to them. It's not a question of apportioning blame – more a question of accepting responsibility for the job you're paid to do!"

"But these cows had this before I came here!" she flared, her sense of righteous indignation getting the better of her.

"Then it was up to you to pinpoint it immediately. Every day is vital. If your training has registered at all, you ought to realise that staphylococci proliferate at an alarming rate. This man could lose some of his herd because of your ineptitude!"

"Well, really! I defy you to make me responsible for what Ron Jordan's employees should have dealt with long before now. How dare you blame me! I only started here a week ago. You have absolutely no right to accuse me!" She flung at him furiously.

He pushed her aside aggressively and she felt the pain as her shoulder was forced against the rails of the milking pens.

"Just don't cross my path again or I shall report you for negligence and make sure you never qualify!"

His dark, angry eyes looked at her fiercely as he passed, defying her to answer him back.

She had stood stunned for some minutes before following him out of the milk parlour, anger and hurt clouding her judgement as her first reaction was to leave the farm. She had endured quite enough of ribald, disgusting comments from the herdsmen and male chauvinism from the farmer. Now the local Vet had her marked down as 'failed' before she could even qualify, and his arrogance had infuriated her. She tried to convince herself that she would be justified in leaving immediately after the attitude she had to contend with, with people trying to intimidate her at every turn. As she rounded the corner of the barn, voices carried across the cool night air.

"You was on'y 'ere not above two weeks ago – you told me then as the 'erd was clean!" Jordan asserted loudly.

"Mr Jordan, anything can happen in that short time. And I did not go all through your herd. If you remember, you were worried about the cost for such a time-consuming job. You know the importance of daily checks and for careful prevention programmes". Sinclair's voice was cold, matter-of-fact.

"My chaps 'ave been partic'lar alright. If it weren't for a slip of a girl, I might not 'ave knowed 'bout it even now!"

29

Caroline was surprised to find that Jordan was defending her. Sinclair, for some reason, was not prepared to admit anything.

"You'd better make sure then that the girl makes no slips! I think you've made a mistake in taking her on. She's hardly had enough experience and training to be relied upon. And girls don't make satisfactory herdsmen! And they don't make good Vets, either, for that matter!" He flung his shoulder as he strode off to his car without giving Jordan time to respond.

Caroline, furious with his attitude, determined to prove Sinclair wrong, as she marched back around the barn to the little caravan which Jordan had provided for her to live in over the summer she was employed at the farm. In his own gruff way, Ron Jordan had shown an appreciation of her vigilance.

"Good job you was keen-eyed enough to notice what my chaps 'ad missed", he admitted to her the day after her unfortunate first meeting with Sinclair. "When that Vet'nary comes in, I'd 'preciate your standin' by".

"I think I'd rather not, under the circumstances", she excused herself, "Mr Sinclair and I would appear to be of ill-matching temperaments – besides, he has already ordered me to stay out of his way".

"Hmph! You city folks is all the same. But mark my words, young lady, out 'ere, in this wildness, there's no place to 'ide from folk. Whether you likes folks or not, you got to abide 'em!"

I'd prefer to be my own judge of the situation", she protested. "If my services are required and asked for, then naturally, I'll be available". In the light of Sinclair's attitude towards her, and despite Ron

Jordan's advice, Caroline felt it in her best interest to be out of sight when he came to visit the farm three days later to check the herd.

Despite her intention to avoid him, Sinclair sent for Caroline.

"Since you're here you might just learn something of practice in the field", he had arrogantly told her as she entered the milking parlour.

"I'm sure I'm more than grateful for any small crumbs of information that might come my way", she said churlishly, piqued by his manner.

He chose to ignore her remark as he injected into one of the quarters of the cow's udder.

"After a herd treatment of this kind, don't forget that the maintenance of a clean herd is most imperative. Dirty hands, dirty stalls, faulty use of the milking machine all encourage the persistence of this disease". He turned to look at her briefly, a flash of contempt in his grey eyes, his dark brows raised scornfully. "You may think you know it all, but unless you follow a routine of cleanliness most assiduously, then this sort of calamity occurs".

"I'm well aware of that, Mr Sinclair, I don't require a lecture", she said trying to keep her irritation under control.

"Don't think for a moment that you know anything yet", he flashed at her, "the real learning and training begins after you leave Vet School". His eyes raked her slender figure. "God knows, you're at a grave disadvantage to begin with. This is no place for females", he taunted, "and you're hardly out of your gymslip!"

"I hardly think that one's sex should come into it", she replied acidly.

"It will, young lady, at calving time. A slip of a girl's not much use then. You should have stuck to city pets".

"I realise you have no time for females in this profession", she amended coolly, not prepared to be roused further by his outrageously chauvinistic attitude.

Alexander Sinclair was undeterred by her indifference and appeared intent upon provoking her further.

"No time at all, Miss Franklin, so don't think you can prove anything to me by fluttering an eyelid or two!"

Caroline took a quick breath, determined not to fall into the trap he was laying. It was pathetic, she mused, how a man, feeling his masculine preserves threatened, will deny a woman's pronounced ability and accuse her of flouting her femininity. They never appear able to accept that a woman can be feminine and capable, she thought.

Caroline had made a deliberate effort to be out of reach whenever Alexander Sinclair came to Jordan's farm again. It was too much to expect that he would ever display professional courtesy to her and whilst she wanted to assert herself she still felt it was prudent to err on the side of caution with a man whose temper might unleash an unpleasant backlash as far as her career was concerned.

Late one night towards the end of her stay at Jordan's, Brian, one of the herdsmen, rapped frantically on the caravan door, his voice a mixture of urgency and fear. One of the cows had decided to drop her calf and was clearly in great distress.

It was now that Sinclair's words came home to her. She was so slight, her arms so short. Struggling to help the cow calve nearly exhausted her.

"Don't forget the mother!" A stern reprimand from the door broke in on them both. "She's worth more than the calf – did you think for a moment to check the cow?" Sinclair gave a faint snort of derision as he strode across the barn to the cow, who by now had struggled back to her feet again after the exhaustion of the calving.

Caroline flinched at his reaction, and without a word to him, carefully lifted up the calf and took it to its mother, who began immediately to lick her offspring.

"Somehow", Caroline held his gaze, "I don't think we need worry", she said defiantly, "But you're the expert, Mr Sinclair, I suggest you make any decisions now that you have arrived".

"I'm sure you've done your best", he replied sarcastically, but I did warn you that a woman is out of her depth in these situations".
His mouth tightened and there was a cruel smile in his arrogant eyes.

"So sorry if I've been in the way", she tossed at him furiously, deeply hurt by his attitude, and she stormed out of the barn and back to her caravan.

Brian called after her but she pretended his voice was lost in the night air. She had not wanted praise from Sinclair – just recognition and a little respect. But that was something which would never be forthcoming from someone like him. Exhausted though she was, it took her a long time to get to sleep and her only consolation as she drifted off was that there were only a few days left at Jordan's farm. She would never have to be confronted by Sinclair again. But she resolved that no-one like him would ever have the opportunity to humiliate her ever again.

Unfortunately for Caroline, Alexander Sinclair had reappeared in her life. She had suffered the indignity of losing the partnership in the Broadway Practice to him. Mr Devine had now advised her to sell out to Sinclair and even her mother seemed to be inclined for her to do so.

Strong as she knew herself to be, Caroline had very lately come to realise some of her own inadequacies. Not the least was the physical strength she lacked. Brain is all very well, she convinced herself, but reflecting back she knew Sinclair's words had been right about pure physical strength. She would never admit it though, not to anyone, and least of all to Alexander Sinclair!

Turning off the hose, she quite involuntarily broke into a sob. It was totally out of character for Caroline, probably self-pity borne of anger and frustration and the whole unhappy situation she now found herself in.

"Oh, Dad", she cried, "Oh, Dad, it was never meant to be like this!"

CHAPTER 3

For a military man, Mr William Franklin's attention to finance had been nothing short of neglectful. The Sanctuary finances had all been eaten away and her father had been dipping into his own capital to keep the day-to-day function going.

"I'm afraid, Miss Franklin, you'll have to demonstrate a little more perspicacity than your father if you intend to pursue the Sanctuary yourself and avoid bankruptcy". Mr Devine tried to convince her of the seriousness of the situation. "I had suggested to your father that he become a registered Charity – that way, fundraising could probably just have kept him in the black. You see", he smiled apologetically, "the animals don't pay for their keep, so unless you can increase the funds from the boarding animals and your hens, then I see you'd be in even more trouble".
He was only trying, Caroline knew that, but the irritation in her voice could not be disguised.

"I'm surprised you let things get so out of hand – I thought you advised my father!"
She was smarting with the knowledge that her father had failed to keep command of the situation. It was uncharacteristic of him, but still the admission hurt her.

Mr Devine was undeterred by her criticism,

possibly even sensing the real motive for it. For months he had pursued Mr Franklin, urging him to keep a firmer control. As an accountant, he had secretly thought the Sanctuary an ill-advised venture financially and certainly one unlikely to yield any profit. As a humanitarian, he admired and respected Mr Franklin and could even recognise that the latter drew more gratification from his work at the Sanctuary than he himself ever obtained from proving a satisfactory balance sheet. He coughed politely.

"Your father was a difficult man to pin down, Miss Franklin – and indeed a man of very independent spirit who heeded his own inclinations". He removed his spectacles, carefully wiping them on the neatly-folded handkerchief. Caroline had watched him do this before and she found it irritating. It was a slow, methodical process, hypnotic in its regularity as his thin voice piped on in the darkening room.

"I'm not suggesting for a moment that he was imprudent – oh no, not at all! Quite the reverse – but his nature did not allow him to say 'No', and the capacity of the Sanctuary was overstretched because of his generosity". She took a deep breath to control her emotions.

"Mr Devine, I aim to run it in a more business-like way". She outlined her plans to him and asked if he had any information on the seeking of Charity status.

"Naturally, I did obtain all the relevant details for your father – and they're still here in the file". He handed her some pamphlets and added, "I take it then, you've made up your mind to decline Mr Sinclair's offer?"

"Nothing would induce me to hand over my

father's dream to a man like Sinclair", she said resolutely.

Mr Devine hesitated a moment, leaned back in his chair, and watching her closely said, "My dear, if you'd take my advice, don't judge Mr Sinclair too harshly. After all, he is only half of the Barron Broadway Practice."

Caroline was quick to respond.

"He and Hugh Morrison are partners – I've seen their bills to my father. I believe they've been responsible for ruining his finances. They've charged him full professional rate, visited him every week from what I can see, purely as a professional call whether treatment was asked for or required or not. They've ruined him!" She finished emphatically.

"I think you'll find….." he tried to interject but Caroline decided she hadn't finished having her say.

"He was probably so distracted over his finances that he never took the proper precautions when he raced into the flaming Cattery that night to save the animals. In a way they may have killed him".

Her voice was raised almost hysterically and Mr Devine gave her anger a moment to subside.

"Well, professionally speaking, it's not for me to say, of course, but – well…." he hesitated.

"Say whatever you wish, Mr Devine, it won't bring my father back", she added somewhat petulantly.

"No, that's true of course, but I think … I think that time will reveal that you have misjudged Mr Sinclair, Miss Franklin, if you don't mind my saying so!"

But Caroline would have none of it.

"Incidentally, did Hugh Morrison make an

offer?" she asked baldly.

He gave another little polite cough.

"More of an insult, Miss Franklin, I did not think it worthy of mention", he apologised. "As a matter of fact the offer did not even cover your father's original capital outlay. However, if you did wish me to follow it through in preference to Mr Sinclair's offer…?"

She shook her head, too exasperated with Hugh Morrison to say anything that would decently fit her feelings.

"Good. There is something though which I should discuss with you and your mother, of course, and that is the Life Policies on your father. It is a very considerable sum of money, and provided it is invested carefully, not, I would add, in the Sanctuary, it should provide your mother with a comfortable pension for the future. She is still a relatively young woman, but starting to earn a living at her time of life would cause infinite problems and distress to her, I'm sure".

Caroline drove back to the Sanctuary still puzzling over Mr Devine's comments about Sinclair and wondered just how insulting Hugh's offer had actually been, and indeed whether Sinclair did know anything about it.

She should have asked the accountant, although, she reflected, he probably would not have wanted to break any professional ethical code. She was relieved at least that her mother would have no financial hardship. Forty thousand pounds – plus her husband's naval pension.

It occurred to Caroline that if her mother was willing to go, she should suggest a stay at her only sister's home in Cornwall. Still, she could let the dust settle first before making that proposal, she thought, pulling off the road into the petrol station to fill up the tank.

"Well, well, I recognised the car not the gorgeous lady driving it", Hugh Morrison followed her into the forecourt and pulled alongside her. Caroline's heart sank. She had managed to avoid Hugh since the funeral.

"It's an unaccustomed pleasure to see you dressed like a woman, instead of a vet!" He slipped an arm around her shoulder affectionately and pecked her on the cheek.

Caroline winced.

"What brings you into this neck of the woods?" His hand slipped from her shoulder and he patted her on the bottom, as one pats a dog or a horse, she thought.

"This and that", she replied non-committally.

"You're not playing vet today, obviously – although I hear you've got yourself lined up with old Briggs at Cheltenham. You'll have to be careful – he likes the ladies".

"I can take care of myself", Caroline asserted, avoiding answering him directly. "How's your practice doing anyway?"

"Oh fine, fine – I'd like to remind you Cal, that I'm only waiting for your word and I'll take care of you on a permanent basis".

His arm tightened around her waist.

Driving away, Caroline shuddered inwardly. Hugh was not every woman's idea of a marriage partner. Very tall, good-looking enough in a basic way, he adopted a slight stoop to counteract his height.

His oddly calculating air had never endeared him to her. But then, she reflected, she had always been spoiled by the example of her father and with any many she ever met, she was trying to find someone who matched up to her father's qualities. Hugh left her wanting. He did absolutely nothing for her physically and she had never given him occasion to think she remotely felt anything for him.

He was pleasant enough company on the odd occasions when she had made the effort to accept an invitation from him, but that had been more to appease her parents who both thought she did not socialise enough. He had once attempted to draw some physical response from her and Caroline, slightly repulsed at his fumbling approach, had coolly put him in his place. Somehow though, Hugh did not appear to have got the message and had pursued her relentlessly on every available opportunity.

Hugh had not mentioned the Sanctuary, nor his offer to buy her out. Curious, though, Caroline reflected, because his sister, Julia, had seen fit to talk about it when they'd met her in Cheltenham. Hugh was not a particularly shrewd man. He was devious, yes. Shrewd, no. Caroline sensed that if she had led him on a little he might have been forthcoming and indeed know something of the Alexander Sinclair offer. She decided to play these local vets at their own game.

Knowing that Hugh would have to ultimately be following behind her, she pulled into the next lay-by. She did not have many minutes to wait and flagged him down.

"Lady in distress, I hope!" he laughed. "It's a good job you're in that fetching little number, Cal and

I hope it's only me you've flagged!"

"No distress, Hugh, it's that I clean forgot back at the garage. I'd intended to ask you over, get a second opinion on something, you know", she lied.

"Why Cal, anytime – you know I'll always be around to help – you only need to shout", he proffered obligingly.

"Perhaps tonight, then – if you've finished surgery in time".

She was anxious to find out as soon as possible what he and Sinclair had been up to. By the time he arrived she would have been able to think up some legitimate reason for calling him over.

Her mother was surprised she had invited Hugh instead of Alexander Sinclair.

"Your father never really valued Hugh's opinions, dear. He always used to talk to Alex when it was something of importance".

"You know my feelings about Sinclair, mother".
In truth, Caroline had never divulged very much to her parents, especially what had happened at Ledbury.

"You can't still hold it against him because Hugh gave him the partnership, surely dear? He is a good vet after all, and" she added quietly, "I don't think he ever charged your father".

"Oh mother, don't be naïve. The vet's bills were enormous", she challenged.

"Yes, but those must have been Hugh Morrison's weekly visits. Your father never asked him to come and he was too polite to stop him. You know he always thought that you and Hugh, well, you never said to the contrary…." her voice trailed off.

"For God's sake, mother! Hugh and me nothing! Do you mean to say that Dad went into financial straits because he couldn't say no to that, that... devious rat, Hugh Morrison. They're partners, anyway. Alexander Sinclair knows exactly what's going on".

Her mother never replied.

"Mr Devine said that Hugh's offer had been an insult. If you ask me it's a put-up job. Hugh offers low then Sinclair slightly higher to make it look like competition. I aim to find out what's been going on, anyway".

Her determination called for no response from her mother.

It was just after eight thirty when Hugh arrived and Mrs Franklin, professing a slight headache had taken herself off to bed long before then. Caroline suspected she couldn't face Hugh Morrison. She didn't much feel like an encounter with him herself, but she was anxious to get to the bottom of things.

But Hugh was not such an easy dupe as she had imagined. Her continued coolness towards him had dampened the edge of his ardour for Caroline. He knew it was too good to be true to be invited so suddenly when she had rebuffed him so often, but he went along with it anyway, just in case there was anything in it for him.

Caroline took him out to the Cattery.

"I'd heard you intended to re-build".

"Word travels fast", she commented dryly.

"Just information in passing, actually, Cal. I treated your builder's Dalmatian yesterday. You know how it is!" He paused. "You're not selling then?" His curiosity got the better of him.

She turned to watch him closely. His thin lips

pursed meanly, his narrow eyes squinted in the light of the bare bulb in the Cattery.

"Was there ever any question of my selling, Hugh?" She asked directly.

There was the faintest trace of guilt as he hedged from one foot to the other.

"Talk – you know – usual gossip…"

She had not trapped him as she had hoped, so she thrust in again.

"No, I'm afraid that Sinclair's offer was simply not good enough". She stabbed.

Hugh was definitely taken aback but he tried to cover it up.

"Well, that's a relief anyway, Cal. It means there's still hope for me, eh?"

"Why, Hugh? Are you offering to buy me out then?" She asked, watching his jaw clench.

"God, me? No, I mean – you and me together Cal. If you sell then you'll go away and then – well – at least, that's a relief you'll not be selling after all", he fumbled.

She had to hand it to him. He had escaped quite well. But she knew now that he was lying. Just like the time when he explained why Alexander Sinclair had been offered the partnership. It was all money, grab and meanness with Hugh Morrison.

What he had never found out was that Caroline had been friendly with the woman who did Hugh's bookkeeping at that time. The figure he charged Sinclair was double what Mr Barron had told Caroline that a partnership in Broadway would cost. She wished the same woman still worked for him now – then she might really find out what was going on.

Unfortunately, her friend had now married and

left the county.

"Well, Cal, good luck to you, I say", Hugh interrupted her thoughts. "I'm glad you asked me over. I was beginning to think the flame had died out between us. Julia will be pleased. She quite likes you, Cal".

Caroline wanted to laugh, but managed to restrain herself.

"We ought to get up a foursome sometime, eh? You and me, my sister and Alex, of course".

The thought made her quake inwardly.

"I'm going to be kept pretty busy for the while, Hugh, running the Sanctuary and developing it and so forth. Not to mention my job with Mr Briggs".

"Well, we'll see anyway – perhaps just the two of us, eh?" He slipped his arm round her waist possessively. "Maybe I can come over and give you a hand?"

"Not if you're intending to charge for your services Hugh". That's how you ruined my father, she wanted to continue. "I'm on a shoestring budget, as I'm sure you must be aware", she added lightly. "Now, I'd value your professional opinion on this, though, if you can give it for free!" And not that I'm even listening or intending to take the slightest bit of notice either, she thought wickedly to herself.

"Ah the Cattery!"

When Hugh left, Caroline felt as if she had gained precious little from the meeting except it was clear that Sinclair had kept his own intentions and his activities to himself. Hugh was still prepared to lie to cover up his own deviousness and clearly the Sanctuary and all its land was still more important to him than Caroline was. Quite probably his only machinations had ever been towards getting his hands on the Sanctuary.

It was more than likely that Alexander Sinclair had exactly the same idea as Hugh. He was more subtle about it. He had played up to her father, whereas Hugh had hoped to win favours with Caroline and marry into the Sanctuary. That way it would cost him nothing. Or were they in league together?

Was Sinclair playing up to her father to win the Sanctuary at a low price what Hugh had crippled him financially?

They must have thought the fire and her poor father's demise were a Godsend.

How wrong they both were!

Damn! She had meant to ask Hugh if he knew anything of Oliver Cory. Oh well, she reflected, it could wait.

It was still quite early so Caroline began to look through the pile of papers in her father's desk. She knew it would cause her mother a lot of pain and yet the paperwork had to be dealt with. Much of it was simply to be filed in the appropriate folders, bills for the accountant to deal with and plenty for the waste bin too!

She had often helped her father in his office on her vacations but this time it felt strange. He was no longer there to advise, suggest or chivvy her along. She was in control now.

Decisions had to be made and Caroline would have to make them.

A letter signed by Alexander Sinclair immediately arrested her attention. It was dated some six months earlier, handwritten, but curiously with an Edinburgh address.

Any qualms Caroline may have had about reading her father's personal mail were quickly dissipated by her own urgency to unravel the mystery of Sinclair's offer and the condition which her father had apparently insisted upon.

The letter however, was not to give her the answer she needed. It was certainly a friendly, chatty letter. Sinclair's handwriting was decisive, well-formed, and positive in its neatness. There was a reference to his Edinburgh address – the death of his mother had necessitated an immediate visit to his home town and he regretted not being able to come over for his 'usual'.

Whatever the 'usual' was, Caroline hadn't a clue. He promised to get in touch the following week. In the last sentence, however, he did refer to "chatting about the future and the pre-condition". He had signed himself 'Yours, Alex'. Significantly, there was a postscript – PS – "Keep an eye on Cory!"

Caroline's imagination was fired.

There was something. And maybe Sinclair knew something about Oliver Cory.

She rifled through the remaining papers hurriedly, anticipating more, but the rest was all mundane and could wait.

The future was very much at the forefront of her mind as she started her letter to Defra. A contact at Cambridge now worked for them and Caroline had been in touch with her University friend to get 'inside' information before putting pen to paper. Quarantine Kennels came under the very strictest of supervision. Planning permissions, local authority sanctions, health regulations – it went on and on. But she knew that if they were to make any headway financially, the battle had to begin. She was under no illusions. It would be a battle. And she felt sure she could expect some opposition from a Kennel and Cattery near Cheltenham since they had been refused permission two years ago.

It would all cost money. Staffing ratios had to be increased. Labour was expensive. Thank goodness she'd a job herself to start the next week.

The Charity status was something to chase up.
It was almost eleven thirty when she finished and decided to take a last look round the Sanctuary.

The kennel maids, who had both agreed to live in the flat over the huge garage, had long turned off their lights. They were both reliable enough but Caroline's instinct told her to check everything was in order, just the same.

"Come on Whistler", she called, taking the torch. When she reached the front door, she switched all the main floodlights on, opened the door and Whistler ran off towards the main gate barking furiously.

At that moment Caroline heard footsteps, a car engine started up on the road outside and the sound of a superior vehicle raced off up towards the village – no lights were switched on on the car though. She was scared out of her wits. With no lights on in the girls' flat it was unlikely that a boyfriend was just late in departing. Still, all the same, she'd ask them in the morning, just to be sure.

Whistler came back to her command, but she was growling, deep in her throat, obviously unhappy with the situation.

When Caroline had lived in Zambia, there had

been many nights when she felt she was living on a knife edge. Attempted poaching in the National Park had been a regular nocturnal hazard. They had frequently shared a guard duty – one which Caroline hated. Despite her status as a Veterinary Surgeon she still felt she was a woman first. She never considered herself well-equipped to defend against marauding poachers who were careless enough with their shots in daylight, let alone in the pitch dark bush country when escape was infinitely easier.

She was tempted now to leave the two guard dogs roaming the compound at night. Although even this precaution could have its hazards. She had heard of expatriates when she was in Zambia, whose guard dogs had been tossed poisoned meat. Within no time the dogs were writing in the last agonies of death, while the house was rifled.

It might prove costly to leave the security lights on all night but perhaps it would be worth it. Anyway, she'd talk to the local constable next day.

Just as she was going in however, the sound of the same engine came racing up the hill from the village and she was sure it was a dark Saab that shot past the main entrance.

It occurred to her that Alexander Sinclair drove a dark Saab.

CHAPTER 4

Some hours later, after an intolerably sleepless night, Caroline was able to satisfy herself that the girls in the flat had received no visitors the previous night. They did admit to hearing Whistler barking though, and both confessed female cowardice at not checking the cause of her disturbance.

"We was both on'y sayin', Miss Franklin , maybe if the lights was on throughout the night – or even if you left a couple of dogs out…"

"Well, I'm loathe to do that, actually, Tracy", Caroline confessed and explained her reasons.

"I see your meaning now, yes, perhaps you're right", Tracy felt her one bright idea had been squashed but immediately managed to come up with another.

"Beg your pardon, Miss Franklin, but me mum and dad use geese. They do cackle if anyone comes nigh. You can keep 'em away from old foxy too, 'cos they could stay in the outer dog run". She seemed well-pleased with her suggestion.

"Brilliant!" Caroline applauded her. "Of course, that's the answer".

Tracy went away beaming.

Caroline told her mother of the proposal.

"She's a good, sound practical girl, that one, Cal.

Her sister will probably be the same given her chance and a little time".

"They're honest anyway, mum. Better to be scared and sensible than filled with false bravado and stupidity".

Caroline had not told her mother the full story of the previous night's episode and especially had not mentioned her suspicions about the car which had whizzed past the entrance.

It was just as well, for ten minutes later with the breakfast things put away, the same car pulled up on the driveway!

Alexander Sinclair strode unhesitatingly up to the rear door, knocked and popped his head round into the kitchen.

"Good morning, ladies. Och! Am I too late for a coffee?"

There was a trace of a smile around his eyes although Caroline imagined there was a hint of tiredness in his face. She was about to refuse him a drink but thought better of it.

"I'm sure that such an early call deserves a reward. Have you been up all night?" She asked with unexpected frankness.

His eyes crinkled in amusement.

"You could say that", he replied, watching Caroline with a thoughtful, narrowed gaze. "You look a bit tired yourself".

His solicitous sneer stunned her.

"Oh, I'm all right – a late night with paperwork, that's all", she admitted, not prepared to give anything away.

Too late, though, for Mrs Franklin's innocuous honesty prevailed.

"Cal said there was someone about last night, Alex".

He inclined his head questioningly towards Caroline, but she stuck to her resolve.

"I think it was nothing, but we'll take precautions, just the same".

He sat down, sprawled his long legs in front of him and eyed her almost suspiciously.

"Geese, Alex – what do you think of that for a defence system, eh?"

Mrs Franklin asked him cheekily.

Caroline was glad to see her mother perking up this morning and endorsed what the latter had said.

"I think it's a splendid idea!"

He sipped his coffee, his cool, grey eyes penetratingly obvious to Caroline. He seemed a huge man in the small chair. His whole presence dominated the kitchen. He was clearly in an affable frame of mind, no acerbity in his voice and a note of genuine sincerity in his conversation.

Caroline found it frankly disarming.

When he rose to give Mrs Franklin the cup, he slipped an appreciative arm around her shoulders, thanking her with what Caroline considered unnecessary vigour just for a cup of coffee! But her mother was not repelled, quite the reverse, in fact. And Caroline felt left out. There was clearly a long-standing warmth between them and something decidedly maternal in response from her mother to Sinclair.

"By the way", he turned to Caroline, "should you need me – in a hurry, that is, - your mother has my car 'phone number. It will get me at any time, day or night", he added.

This honesty and candour from him was so unexpected. There had been an inflection in his words which sent a shiver over her skin. There was a look in his eyes which sent alarm licking through her veins.

His arm was still around her mother's shoulder in filial affection. For those few moments Caroline felt excluded from their intimacy. It had never occurred to her that Sinclair might also have made a friend of her mother and not simply her father. Something in his treatment of her suggested an understanding between them, a friendship of long-standing.

In a way, Caroline was embarrassed. How many times had she ranted on about that Alexander Sinclair and her mother had weakly defended him without making Caroline feel that she could be in the wrong. With his arm still around her mother he reached towards Caroline and curled his other arm possessively around her waist.

"There now, ladies – warmth, congeniality and all topped by a splendid coffee!" Caroline was silenced by the glint in his eyes but more by the heat from his body pulsing against her.

"What more could a man ask for?" he entreated, his eyes boring into Caroline at such close range. His hot breath brushed so close to her cheek she sensed he felt the heat flooding through her.

"Now", he declared, releasing them both, "no question about it – any late callers lurking about, you buzz me right away. I can be here in seconds. Which reminds me, Caroline, I came to congratulate you – you'll be working for a very good friend of mine".

This complete change of stance from Sinclair left her totally dumbfounded. She had genuinely been unable to pinpoint anything he said (or did, in fact), and respond with her brand of caustic animosity. While he was in such affable humour, she decided to test him.

"By the way, Mr Sinclair, I … that is, we … we decided to refuse your offer. I've no doubt Mr Devine our accountant will be in touch".

There, she thought, that'll throw him off balance.

But it didn't.

"Yes, he spoke to me yesterday – although, I, we, had naturally felt that you would refuse, of course. I admire your tenacity. It may well be misplaced but I respect it just the same".

He turned obstinately from Caroline and quite deliberately led her mother out to his car, his arm linked through hers. She was unable to hear what was said between them and Caroline felt it inappropriate to question her mother directly. She didn't have to, however.

"He's been such a friend to us – me and your father, Cal, I know you've your own reasons for not wanting him to come near the place, but I want you to understand that Alex has free access here. It would have displeased your father greatly if you had shown yourself hostile to Alex".

"Point taken, mum. Only don't expect me to swoon over him, will you? A woman in my position does not take kindly to being insulted by a professional colleague, especially in front of other staff. Something like that I can never forgive". She felt she had to put her mother slightly more in the picture.

"Well, Cal, dear, that's something for you to worry about and he may have had his reasons – oh, I know what you're thinking, that I'm defending him. Yes, well, what if I am. He's a fine Vet, a good friend and certainly more of a man of integrity than his weedy partner". She flushed excitedly. "There, I've said it now. I'll never say it again, but I don't like Hugh Morrison", she said emphatically, placing herself firmly in the chair.

Caroline laughed.

"Oh, mum, really? Thank goodness for that", she added lightly. "I honestly thought you had lined me up with him for a long-term match!"

"God forbid, child!" her mother tutted, "now, where are those two kennel girls?"

Caroline took her 'bag of tricks' as her mother called it, and went to check over the cats. Some of them had died in the fire but most of them had had a lucky escape – at the expense of her father's life. One or two of them still had wheezy coughs but nothing Caroline's ministrations couldn't cure. On the way back she stopped off to look at the re-building of the new Cattery.

"Mornin', Miss Franklin", Mr Gabriel the builder was hard at it.

"Good morning, John, nice work, it's coming on fast".

"Tis easy, this one. Like I said – on'y a matter o' days really. All your foundations is good, see. Them cats'll be back in 'ere 'fore next week, m'dear", he replied cheerily.

"I wish everything else would move as quickly, John".

"Oh, Time, my dear, is the devourer of things". She was surprised at him quoting Ovid.

"You did Latin, John?"

"Not me, missis – but I knows a bit when I see it 'cos my old dad used to quote 'en often enough. An' you mark my words, 'tis true we're all eaten up by Time in the finish. Don't do to 'urry to the Gates, m'dear, 'cos once you'm through 'tis too late!"

"Very true, John", she laughed, "I'll try and remember to slow down!"

Even so, Caroline was pragmatic enough to realise that a job done today was one fewer to do tomorrow. She would only have a few days left to organise as much as she could before beginning to take on her first full-time veterinary job in England.

It cheered her little enough to know that even twenty miles away she couldn't escape Sinclair or his influence. No doubt he had warned his friend Avery Briggs about her.

She was not exactly looking forward to it, but was more than grateful for his apparent readiness to take her on. It would give them a fighting chance to retain the Sanctuary.

Another source of income, though little enough, would be the winter grazing she had consented to for a local farmer. A few hundred sheep would be lost in the Franklin acres throughout the Autumn and Winter and still leave Caroline plenty of scope for whatever else she had in mind.

In the meantime she had to get to the printers in Evesham. One idea of raising money was through sponsorship and pledges with local schools. She had drafted a leaflet to circulate within the locality. Her next plan was to get local radio to give her a quick publicity spot to help boost support and interest. But Charity status was the first hurdle and she was pleased she had got her letters done the previous night so they could be posted straight away in Evesham. Before she left, though, a quick word with John Gabriel might lead to some geese.

He was a local man and knew everybody's business for twenty miles around. She was right, and he was able to point her in the right direction for her geese.

"By the way, missis, I meant to tell 'e earlier, that vet'nary Morrison were asking after you t'other day". Intrigued, Caroline allowed him his gossipy way.

"Ah, 'e were quite quizzical, if you knows my meanin'? 'Ow long 'afore the job'd be done? Was it costin' much? Was Miss Franklin for sellin' up?"

"And what did you say, John?"

"Well, 'e'd just done my Trixie, my damnation, as the wife calls 'er, so I 'ad to be civil like. But I on'y told 'en as we was doing the Cat 'ouse. I thought 'e was sweet on you Miss, but I reckon you'd 'ave told 'en answers to all they questions".

"Quite right, John, quite right", she laughed.

"I told 'en as you never talks to 'ole John Gabriel: see, I spun a yarn, like, more a kinda web, really. 'E'll get caught by 'is own mischief I've no doubt, eh", he roared loudly, pleased at his own little brand of cleverness, and then carried on laying the breeze blocks.

A couple of nights later Caroline was unable to sleep and went to fetch some milk from the kitchen. Two of the outside security lights were on and sufficient light was cast through the drawn curtains for her to see without putting on the kitchen light. Whistler was lying by the door growling low in her throat. She knew someone was about outside. Caroline wished to goodness the geese had arrived, as promised. Unfortunately the man who was bringing them had had his van break down and they wouldn't arrive until the next morning. Caroline urged Whistler on.

"Go, fetch 'em, girl, who's there?" she whispered urgently to the dog.

Whistler's growls became a furious barking. Caroline switched on the two remaining security lights which flooded the main compound and cast a shadow across a man running towards the main gate.

Caroline's first thought was Sinclair. He had said to ring if anyone was about. Although she was quaking, she decided not to 'phone him. That would be playing right into his lap. He wanted them to be dependent on him.

She was sure of that. It strengthened his hand against Caroline. A woman, afraid at night, unable to cope. It would confirm his argument for the selling – despite his comments to her in front of her mother a couple of days earlier.

Just then a car drew up on the driveway, headlights blazing through the drawn curtains. She wrapped her dressing gown tightly around her and peeped out to see Alexander Sinclair. He turned off the lights and engine and must have seen the movement of the curtain for he came across and tapped gently on the window.

Not doubting it was him, she opened the door.

Whistler jumped up and down sniffing and tail-wagging with obvious delight.

Caroline was only pleased that she did not have to offer such over-displays of gratitude.

"I was only passing and I saw all your lights on", he explained in a whisper. "Have you had any trouble?" he asked closing the door quietly behind him.

"But it's two in the morning", Caroline stuttered, "what on earth are you doing passing by here at this time of night – or rather morning?"

"I'm on night duty", he brushed off her query. "Why are all the lights on? I thought you were getting the geese?" he asked in a conspiratorial whisper.

"A van breakdown, I'm afraid, they're due tomorrow, well, today now, seeing as it is already past midnight!" she fumbled on, conscious of his eyes raking over her body in the half light. "I just came down for a drink."

"Well now you're down, I'll have one as well, Caroline. It's a cool night out there, even though it's supposed to be summer." His eyes lingered on the rapid rise and fall of her breasts beneath the too-thin dressing gown.

"You know you ought not to go about dressed like that, it makes a man's blood flow in his veins". There was an enigmatic gleam in his eye.

She was intensely aware of his maleness and shivered with apprehension. She couldn't cope with this kind of manner from Sinclair. She felt uneasy with his affability and decided she was far safer, as a woman, when he behaved like the arrogant chauvinist she had first met in Ledbury.

He switched on the kitchen light and filled the kettle for her. She seemed rooted to the spot.

"Are you sure you're all right?" He asked.

She was simply appalled by the instinctive leaping of her senses. Her eyes dwelt hungrily on the muscular breadth of his shoulders tapering to the lean waist and powerful legs. He was dressed only in slacks and a light sweatshirt which clung to the ripple of muscles across the expanse of chest.

He knew. She felt instinctively that he knew.

He stepped forward and pulled her in towards his body, warm and strong.

"My God, you're half frozen to death. You've had a shock, Caroline", he murmured.

The ineffable warmth seeped into her and she was grateful that he simply thought she had had a shock. She leaned into him, her body feeling tiny and fragile encircled by his powerful arms. Her head rested against his chest and the sweet maleness of him overpowered her. Heat flooded through her and she felt giddy and light-headed with the sheer joy of being held.

"You need a good hot drink, young lady", the deep Scottish drawl caused a tingling sensation in her neck. If he had not supported her she would have collapsed like a rag doll.

His hand cradled her head and he pulled her closer to him. His breath was warm against her cheek.

"Come on, Caroline", he urged, "you've nothing to be afraid of now".

She pressed instinctively again as his mouth moved against her skin.

"I'll be all right", she squeaked, "there was a … a man … he ran across towards the gate … I … I'm sorry, I feel so feeble".

"But ye are feeble", he lapsed into his vernacular accent, "ye're no but a wee wench, for a' tha's a clever brain. Sit ye down, I'll brew ye a strong tea".

She was glad of the seat now. The weakness was past. Had he known the truth? She wondered peeping at him through her fingers as she rested her head in her hands.

Caroline could easily despise herself for that weakness, that sudden succumbing to his maleness. How he would laugh at her if he knew. The clever Caroline was as weak as water, like putty in his hands. He, who said women Vets ought to stick to domestic pets. Sinclair, who had usurped her place in the Broadway Practice. He had wheedled his way into the affections of her parents, even made them an offer for the business they ran and dearly loved. It was the same character.

She instinctively loathed chauvinists like him. There had been a few over the years and it was not the first time that Caroline had encountered opposition – especially from men in the profession. What was it that gave them the right to assume their supremacy in the handling of animals?

Caroline resented Sinclair more for his attitude towards the female vet than his chauvinistic attitude towards her simply as a woman. Now she loathed herself for having such wanton thoughts towards him. With any luck he would never know.

She had to make sure of that. He could go on believing she had been scared to death by whoever it was dashing across the grounds at two in the morning.

"There", he said, putting a mug of hot tea in front of her, "that'll do the trick. It certainly will for me, anyway".

"Thank you", she murmured gratefully. "I'm so sorry, Mr Sinclair, it's all been a bit of a shock".

"Yes, I'm sure it has", he agreed, his cool gaze containing a hint of amusement. "However, get the geese out there and they'll scare him half to death – whoever it is".

"I've spoken to the local constable but he's not too optimistic about being able to keep watch. There are only two men for the whole ten mile radius and they work split shifts as it is".

The tea was warming her through and she felt more in control of her emotions now as they began to discuss security.

She explained about her days and the terrifying nights she had spent in Zambia. He was impressed. She meant him to be. It gave her an opportunity to assert herself more.

"Have you worked abroad, Mr Sinclair?"

"Och, no!" he said emphatically, and then added with a laugh, "unless you count England, and that's abroad for many a Scot, I'll have you know!"

She was relieved that he left soon after and that her lapse into his arms appeared forgotten.

Deciding to leave all the security lights on she locked up and felt safer taking Whistler up to bed with her. Whistler didn't object, naturally. But it was a long time before Caroline went to sleep. The car engine sound driving away had definitely been the same as she had heard two nights previously.

The fact actually disturbed her even more than the fact that there was obviously someone prowling about. It could not be a coincidence that Sinclair was out on this lonely road at such an untimely hour. What was he doing? Was he the figure she had seen dashing across the compound?

If that was the case, then what was he hoping to achieve by it?

Was this all part of a game he was playing to win

the Sanctuary by foul means since the fair means had eluded him?

Once again she asked herself if it were possible that he and Hugh Morrison could be in league together to drive her out.

Surely the same man who held her mother with such filial affection could not have designs on destroying her family?

Even the feelings he had aroused in her so recently, surely a genuinely decent man could not … no … the thought was too awful.

And there was Hugh. What did John Gabriel mean when he said that Hugh Morrison would be caught by his own mischief? What did John know? Was it all just supposition?

Caroline's head was spinning. She realised just how vulnerable they were, so isolated like this on the far fringe of the village with the nearest neighbour more than half a mile away. She didn't even know who the nearest neighbour was!

Now there's an admission, she reflected. And where did Sinclair live? Her mother had the 'phone number but she hadn't thought to ask her where he actually lived. It was something she had never been inquisitive enough to find out. It was a fact which was irrelevant, really. Not having been around much anyway during the last three or four years since he stole her place at the Broadway Practice, it had been of no consequence.

Caroline did make one decision though. She wouldn't hold it against him any longer for the partnership he had gained instead of her. She was beginning to reckon she was well out of it anyway.

Her mother shook her awake.

"Cal, whatever's happened to you? It's past nine o'clock!" Mrs Franklin was agitated to say the least. "There's Mr Gabriel's friend with a dozen geese cackling about downstairs. I'm surprised the noise never woke you. The day's half over!"

The day had begun for Caroline at two o'clock that morning, only she had no intention of telling her mother anything about it. She'd go all soppy and, "What a nice man Mr Sinclair is!" she'd say.

Her mother never stopped to analyse. The trouble with Caroline was that the scientist in her made her analyse everything and everyone. Nothing could or should be taken for granted. There is a logical reason for things. A disciplined training is hard to break and Caroline valued her training more than most.

However, the kennel maids had both already made an early report to Mrs Franklin. They had seen a man. Then Mr Sinclair's car was on the compound. After about half an hour his car had left. Such probity!

Oh well, Caroline admitted, at least she needn't keep it back from her mother. She hated any form of deceit and her motive really had been to protect her mother and stop her from worrying.

Anyway they would all be able to feel safer now with the geese cackling about at night.

Whistler wasn't too enamoured though and kept making darts towards a couple of the geese then backing off when the hissing and cackling started up!

The printer in Evesham had run off all the handbill posters and offered to drive over with them but Caroline preferred to make the journey stopping off on the way to do a little shopping in Broadway.

She never bought many clothes, choosing a few select, quality items for special occasions. Most of the time, because of her line of work she practically lived in cords and tee shirts. Caroline knew she wouldn't win prizes as a model – that wasn't her intention. She liked to be comfortable, practical and functional. Because of her light colouring and slender frame, she looked good in most things, but was particularly fond of pinks, lemons and peachy colours. Knowing she would have to try on clothes today she had taken more care with her outfit choosing a light pink two-piece in cotton and silk.

It clung where it touched, revealing the soft curves and delicate bone structure of her svelte five feet five. The small heeled shoe gave sufficient lift to her height and at the same time accentuated the very slender, shapely legs.

Dressed like this Caroline almost felt like a Jekyll and Hyde character as she got into her car and she remarked to her mother.

"I don't feel like a Vet at all, dressed up like this. Strange, isn't it, how clothes are capable of influencing your character!"

"You grew up in cords and tee shirts, Cal. It's about time you discarded them once in a while", her mother admonished gently.

"Yes, but I couldn't do a proper job of work dressed up like this, now could I?"

"Perhaps you shouldn't think of working quite so much, my dear. You've never had a social life".

"Plenty of time for that in the future, mum", Caroline smiled.

"Your father and I always tried to urge you not to work so hard. You've got to have some fun sometimes, Cal dear. Alex was only asking me the other day..."

"Don't start involving me with him", Caroline blurted out. "No way, no thank you, mother! I can do without 'les liaisons dangereuses'!".

"Whatever do you mean, Cal? He only asked if you and Hugh were serious together".

"God!" she fumed, "it's none of his damned business. I hope you didn't tell him anything".

"I can't tell untruths, dear, you know that", her mother replied simply.

She had no right to get do worked up with her mother. She knew that and she promised herself to try and see life from her mother's perspective in future. So long as Alex Sinclair was not in the view finder, then that would be fine. From now on she must keep her distance from him. How easily he had captivated her emotions.

At the high-class outfitter in Broadway she treated herself to a couple of classic lined trouser suits for work. That should look a bit tidier than her cords, she thought, mentally trying to appease her mother. A light-weight woollen dress in emerald came next. A leisure suit in peach was soft and quite flattering, clinging where it touched, leaving little to the imagination! She deliberately tried to appear nonchalant as the cashier told her the total price. Her head swimming, she left the shop reflecting that her first month's salary would be on her back!

Getting back into her car she felt happy and light-hearted, looking forward to her first job in England.

Her mood was soon turned to one of shock though as she saw Hugh Morrison's car parked outside the Lygon Arms. Leaning in through the driver's window talking to Hugh was none other than Oliver Cory!

Caroline stopped in her tracks. She slid down in the seat and watched as Hugh pulled a thick envelope from his inside pocket and then handed it to Oliver Cory. Hugh then drove off in the opposite direction out of the village.

CHAPTER 5

Too much of what Caroline suspected was, in fact, only conjecture. There was little proof of anything. Even the passing of an envelope from Hugh Morrison to Oliver Cory could be perfectly legitimate.

Her brain worked overtime all the way back to the Sanctuary. One idea was tossed in the frame, then another and so on. She desperately needed someone to talk to about the whole situation, but it must be someone she could talk to objectively. The local constable had in fact suggested she might be over-reacting, so there was not much hope for a satisfactory conversation with him.

Her mother and the kennel maids were too involved. John Gabriel was a bit too loose-lipped. Sinclair was suspect, if she had to tell the truth, since she was concerned about his motives.

There was nothing for it. She would simply have to watch and wait and just see how things developed. Typical scientific approach, she snorted to herself!

Monday came quickly enough and Caroline presented herself for action at the Avery Briggs Practice in Cheltenham.

Avery Briggs was a huge bull of a man. Tall, a

heaviness which was exaggerated by the Scottish Tweeds he insisted on sporting – even in warm weather – bespectacled and ruddy-faced, he had a jovial and affable manner which Caroline was attracted to. She was to be perpetually amused by his insistence on wearing a Norfolk deerstalker's hat, whatever the weather.

It was his contention that much heat was lost through his head and as he remarked, "Being a canny Scot, I'll no waste a thing! If I'm to be hot-headed, that's my affair".

Caroline made it a habit not to give a dog a bad name and always took people as she found them. As she shook his hand warmly she couldn't help remembering what Hugh Morrison had told her. "You'll have to be careful – he likes the ladies".

Somehow she couldn't imagine Avery Briggs as a philanderer and wondered where such scurrilous gossip ever emanated.

He had a lively sense of humour and one characteristic which Caroline really appreciated in him was his ability to laugh at himself. He was human – full of rollicking stories of his student days, exploits when he was 'serving his apprenticeship', as he put it.

"Oh ay, Caroline – you're green for the first couple of years".

Someone else had said that to her and she pushed the thought to the back of her mind.

The practice was modest. He preferred it that way.

"Alex tells me you're pretty adept at the back end of a cow!" he guffawed, but not in a way which embarrassed Caroline. She knew that Sinclair must have discussed her, but somehow, with this man, she felt so at ease. He wasn't laughing at her, ridiculing her in any way.

"Oh that", she replied dismissively, "I've had more experience around rhinos than cows, to tell you the truth!"

"Och, I like it!" he burst forth into a peal of warm laughter. "Alex did tell me a bit about you, as it happens. In fact he gave you a damned fine reference before I ever met and interviewed you Caroline".

She was taken aback.

He obviously read her mind.

"Think nothing of it – he's a close friend of your family, I gather. He only makes a few friendships, does Alex, but they're usually good, lasting ones. And incidentally, I'm not coming out with all the clichés about your father. We'll talk at length in the future on that score. Anyway, my dear, your credentials are first class, but unfortunately I can't promise you the wildlife ye've been used to!" he laughed again.

Caroline was to become very accustomed to his easy amusement.

"I'll fit in with whatever you can lay on for me", she joined in readily. "I've been trained to handle anything from a hen to a hippo!"

"Och, we're going to get on fine", he slapped his thigh heartily, beaming at Caroline.

To start with, he had not exaggerated. His practice was confined to the domestic scene regarding animals, although considerable equine work was involved. She spent a lot of time dealing with cats, dogs and other pets, made numerous house calls and ran the surgery much of the time.

Avery Briggs loved horses. In fact he selfishly took over the bulk of the equine patients, and admitted to Caroline that he couldn't help himself.

"I gave up a lot of my other work – I'm not the only Vet in town, for goodness sake! Once you've seen one cow deliver, you've seen enough", he roared. "No, seriously, Caroline", he confessed one day, a week later, "there is no finer creature than a horse. 'Tis a magnificent beast. Personally, I grieve when I have to put one down – which is too often, if the truth be told. Such power and yet grace and beauty. When I'm reincarnated, I'll come back as a horse", he mused.

"But such a short life span in human terms", Caroline reminded him.

"Oh, aye, but I could stand out all night and no' be nagged by anyone. I'd be a magnificent creature instead of this huge ungainly beast I am now!"

He took her to the Cheltenham Racecourse at every available meeting. He knew everyone, acknowledged most people and always displayed a wonderful sense of bonhomie whenever she was with him. He didn't go to the races because he was particularly a betting man. He simply loved to watch horses.

"I've asked Alex Sinclair to join us for the meeting at Cheltenham today", he sprung on her. "He's another horse man, you see. It's in our Scottish blood. If he's not careful he'll end up like me – tethered to a horse and not a woman".

"I thought he was tethered to Julia Morrison", Caroline flung in quite casually.

"My God, don't ever mention that wanton little tart in my hearing", he spluttered over his coffee she had just handed him.

"Sorry, did I say something wrong?"

He placed his cup on the table in front of him.

"Sit ye down, Caroline Franklin. I've a tale that'll

70

no' take long – but if you and I are to remain friends then we'd best straighten the cloth in front of us".

She complied and waited.

"A number of years back now, a young woman was introduced to me, professing to be keen on horses and the like. I won't embarrass you with the detail but let it be enough to say I'm a God-fearing man, and I hope, a gentleman. The wench was after my money – and ther's no' many a Scot will stand a woman wi' her hands in his pockets, if you get my drift. She was an empty-headed wench, indeed and physically she left me cold. I prefer a horse any day. She slandered me and libelled me in a spiteful way – I had to talk to her family about her. As I said, I'm a God-fearing man. If Sinclair is fool enough to pick up fluff from the floor, which I very much doubt, then he'll find it just blows away on a windy day! Anyway, it's no' my line of country to tell another man, especially a Scot, how to behave or run his life!"

"I understand perfectly, Mr Briggs, and I am sorry".

"Ach, you didn't know – but we need never to touch on that raw nerve again, eh?"

She was grateful to him for his honesty. It was consonant with her own views of Julia Morrison anyway, and secretly she thought that if Sinclair had taken up with her, then it served him right.

It was one way he'd certainly get his come-uppance.

Because Sinclair was a close friend of Avery Briggs, it was a fair bet that Julia Morrison wouldn't have been invited along as Sinclair's guest to the races, and Caroline consoled herself with that thought.

For the rest of the morning, trying to put the

afternoon from her mind, Caroline attended to all the surgery animals and then went out on a few visits.

Something had changed in Alexander Sinclair. In fact, to Caroline's mind it almost appeared like a complete character change! Her first encounters with him had been at Ledbury while she was still a student. He had behaved appallingly to her. He had been the epitome of rudeness and arrogance. In Caroline's eyes he was the archetypal, chauvinistic, aggressive male. He had made it quite clear that there was no space in his life for women Vets, unless they just tended cats and dogs. His manner towards her had been strictly unprofessional, most ungracious and unforgivable.

Although it no longer bothered her, he had been responsible for her altering the whole course of her life after University. It was perhaps an injustice to blame him totally – it had been Hugh who welched on a promise. Quite probably Alexander Sinclair had had no idea when he bought into the Broadway Practice that there was someone else likely to be an interested party. Hugh would have kept his cards close to his chest.

Subsequent meetings, on her infrequent returns to the UK had had all the trademarks of veiled hostility on either side. At first she suspected he resented her. She had obtained a First in her degree and gone to spend long stays abroad, undertaking poorly-paid but extremely interesting work. Her research work had resulted in two papers written and presented to international Veterinary magazines. She had taken it all in her stride. A truly accomplished background.

And yet Sinclair had given the impression that

she was a schoolgirl upstart, fresh out of gymslip and socks! He appeared to place no credibility on her training and qualifications.

In the last few short weeks however, his attitude had changed to one of magnanimity. His politeness had been disarming. His interest had stretched to late night calls. Her mother knew him more than she was prepared to say and he, for his part, had shown himself so courteous, warm and friendly towards her mother that Caroline had sometimes felt left out. Twice in the last weeks she had deliberately declined his invitation to go for dinner. Strong in her memory was the physical need he had aroused in her, late one night. Whether he was conscious of his effect on her she could not quite determine.

Her own determination had centred on not giving him any quarter or leeway and no opportunity to try his tactics again. She was so suspicious of his intentions it left her unable to trust whatever he said or did. How could she allow herself to give in to the kind of physical and emotional domination he was capable of exerting over her?

No! She had resolved never to submit to that kind of intimidation. It would go against the grain of everything she had stood for and battled for in the last few years.

Most of the afternoon at the races, Caroline had no cause to fault Alexander Sinclair. To her relief he had spent most of his conversation time and attention with his old friend. She had had plenty of opportunity to observe him though and was not altogether confident that she would have the strength to resist him if he exerted any pressure on her.

"How are you Caroline?"

He had proffered his hand warmly on meeting.

"Fine, thank you, Mr Sinclair".

He was cool and relaxed, wearing light grey, hip-hugging slacks and a cream jersey shirt, slightly open at the next to reveal the curl of dark hair across his broad expanse of chest. His face, lightly tanned, evidenced the amount of time he spent out of doors. He would, of course, Caroline instantly mused, attending to all those huge animals that women Vets should leave alone! She found it more sensible to think badly of him because in fact she found him so attractive. Was that why she had studied him so carefully throughout the afternoon?

"The geese are doing a good job, I gather?" he queried, his voice deceptively mild.

"Whether they have cleared the problem or are merely acting as a deterrent for the moment, I can't decide", Caroline responded.

"Does it matter – so long as they keep you safe?" he asked, his eyes hardening.

"Of course it does", came her quick retort. "I've yet to reassure myself that I'm safe. I'd be more interested to know who was prowling about, and why. Putting a stop to them is the secondary affair. Deterring them is not enough for me, Mr Sinclair. People find a way around deterrents, don't you agree?"

Impressed by her logical train of thought, he told her so.

"I do have some ideas though, of course", she admitted.

"Then you should take up my offer of dinner one evening and we'll talk it over. You've refused me twice already", he gave her a helpless glance.

"I've been very, very busy, as I'm sure you'll be aware", she retorted.

"I think I know your movements better than most", he confided, an intimacy creeping into his voice. "However, I am a gentleman, and a gentleman only asks three times. After that, rejection would be insupportable", he pleaded.

"Then how can I refuse you?" she weakened, all her earlier resolve suddenly dissipated.

"Thank you. I'd hoped to have a long chat with you – no strings – strictly business, I promise".

He placed his hand on his chest in a mock gesture.

Caroline arranged for Mrs Wilkins from the village to make a call on her mother during the evening she went out to dinner with Alexander Sinclair. Knowing full well she would have her mother's complete blessing to go out, especially with Sinclair, Caroline also was aware that her mother would be lonely and probably concerned at being left on her own. Thankfully no more incidents had occurred regarding the late night prowlers, but Caroline erred on the side of caution.

"Oh do come in, Mrs Wilkins, how lovely of you to call", she winked conspiratorially. "Mr Sinclair and I are about to go out for a while, but I'm sure mother will be delighted to see you".

Caroline's mother had no idea of the pre-arranged visit and was secretly overjoyed that her evening would not be spent alone after all.

"You're crafty but caring Caroline", Sinclair murmured to her as they closed the front door.

"It's your fault", she admonished good-humouredly, "if you had not insisted on dinner..."

"Ah well, I have my reasons", he promised, urging the car speedily up the hill out of the village. "As a matter of fact I can't take you where I'd really like to – we haven't the time – it would leave it too late getting back to your mother and I fear Mrs Wilkins' stay will not be too long".

"Where are we going then?" she glanced at him, anticipation in her voice.

"As far from the locality to avoid gossips but near enough to get back in a hurry if your mother rings", he replied confidently, not taking his eyes off the road. "Don't worry, lass, I've got the matter all in hand", he exaggerated his Scots brogue. "Not terribly original, though, I'm afraid, Caroline", he said, glancing at her.

When he pulled up outside the expensive restaurant in Stratford half an hour later, Caroline had no qualms about his choice of venue.

They ordered starters of scallops with lobster and prawns in saffron sauce.

"I'm teetotal when driving, Caroline", he admitted, "but I'd like to offer you wine, if you'll not mind drinking alone".

"If you don't mind, I'll have the Perrier water with lime", she responded.

Already she had found her resolve to be distant and cool was weakening. He was simply too well-behaved for her to respond with anything but pleasantness and warmth. If she dangerously added wine to her menu for the evening, on top of the Martini and ice she'd already drunk then she might not be able to be responsible for her own behaviour.

She found him devastatingly attractive in the half-light of the restaurant. The table was small, the seating was intimate and he felt altogether too close for comfort. He had been watching her with a thoughtful, narrowed gaze whenever she looked up from her food.

"We'll have the supreme of chicken", he instructed the hovering waiter. He was positive, no asking, he'd decided – on everything it seemed and Caroline wasn't sure whether she appreciated having all her decisions made in this way.

Alexander Sinclair must have sensed her thoughts.

"I won't apologise for taking the upper hand, Caroline. It's expediency – besides, I know from your mother that you love chicken! Yes, I've cheated a bit!" He admitted, laughter lines creasing the corners of his eyes.

"Will I at least be able to refuse the treacle pie in preference for the apple pie and cream?" she pleaded with amusement. "No seriously, I don't mind, mum's right – I'm fairly traditional and plain in my eating habits".

"But you're far from plain in any other way, Caroline", he murmured, his gaze intently burning into her.

His unexpected frankness brought a touch of colour to her cheeks.

"And you still blush, which is a pleasure to behold in a woman". He reached out to take her hand in his and stroke the skin tenderly, the warmth of his touch raising goose bumps up her arms. She stiffened slightly and he sensed her tension.

"You're a lovely woman, Caroline", he murmured thickly across the small expanse of table.

She was terrified at the accelerated response to her emotions and her defences sprang to the fore.

"But a lousy Veterinary Surgeon!" she cut in with acid denunciation.

His mouth tightened.

"Your professional status has nothing to do with your being a woman", he replied steadily.

"You surprise me – not a few years ago you decried the whole species of female Vets".

"Caroline, please, you're not making this easy for me", he begged. "Disparaging remarks which I made are purely of historical consequence. We've both come a long way since then".

"Mud sticks, don't you agree, though?" she charged him.

"Och, Caroline, would a profound apology not make you feel easier?"

"It might", she conceded, "but I'd be very suspicious of your motives", she added honestly.

"Okay – for the rest of the evening, can we call a truce? You're still a lovely woman, I've enjoyed having dinner with you, but now I want to talk business".

"Whose?" she asked coolly.

"Yours", he replied frankly.

Caroline leaned back in her chair, trying very hard to conceal the quickness of her breathing.

"Tell me to mind my own business if you feel inclined", he began.

"I probably will", she replied tartly.

"Fair enough. I want to put my cards on the table, Caroline".

She quaked inwardly.

"I made an offer on the Sanctuary for personal reasons which I needn't go into. Your father accepted".

"I don't believe it…" she cut in quickly, her fury rising suddenly.

"Och, I knew you'd react like that – let me go on, please – hear me out before you jump down my throat", he whispered.

People on the next table had already cast a few glances in their direction.

The waiter brought coffee.

"Your father accepted", he repeated and continued, "but only on certain conditions. Even that is no longer relevant. I did though make a formal offer to Mr Devine after Bill's, sorry, your father's death".

"I know that", she said impatiently, waiting for him to come to the point.

"I want you to know and believe that my offer was made at exactly the terms, the conditions aside of course, which your father had previously verbally accepted".

"Well?"

"Caroline, don't be so restive – give me a chance, please", he pleaded.

"I'm sorry – go on".

"When I made the offer to Mr Devine I had no idea you intended to carry on. I've already told you that I admire your tenacity. I do, most sincerely. You've made a very serious decision – you've taken one hell of a lot on. Caroline, I have to say this and I don't mean to be a chauvinistic pig – you're a woman and …"

"I thought we'd get back to that part of it", she cut in contemptuously. "So you think I can't cope? Do you still think I'm a slip of a girl fresh out of my gym slip? I should have stuck to city pets!"

She taunted him with the same words he had used at Ledbury. They were burned into her mind.

"I thought we'd agreed a truce on historic conversations", his eyebrows arched in unconcealed irritation. "You're behaving just like a woman!" he laughed at his own choice of words. "My God, you ought to – you're a fine woman too!"

The tense atmosphere was eased immediately.

"I'm sorry, Mr Sinclair", she was immediately filled with remorse.

"Please stop calling me that – I'm Alex to my friends", he implored.

She sighed. Under different circumstances she'd have called him whatever he wanted.

"I'm worried that the two of you – on your own up there. The village is dead at night. A few geese won't stop another fire burning, Caroline. Do you begin to understand me?"

"What do you suggest?"

"There is so much that I could, so much that I daren't, not yet. What I am asking you is to be alert to the fact that there could be, still, some considerable danger for you alone up at that Sanctuary. We can't pinpoint anything. We've no proof of anything either but I'm afraid I can only suggest we have to wait. In the meantime you have to be very much on your guard. Very alert. Suspicious".

"Oh I'm that all right", she interjected.

"You've good cause to be. But please don't be suspicious of me. I'm on your side".

"And do you still want to buy the Sanctuary?" Caroline asked baldly.

He hesitated and eyed her narrowly, the grey eyes saying nothing.

"Is it still for sale?" he hedged.

"Say if it were", she lied.

"Well, then I've no doubt that if it were then ... there would be a considerable amount of searching to do to give you an honest answer".

Because she knew he was avoiding being direct, she already had seeds of mistrust about him again.

"You're not being straight with me, Alex", she pouted.

"Well, let's say I'd look into it, on certain conditions", he admitted.

"Those conditions seem to have risen their head again. What were they?"

"It's irrelevant now. In any case, conditions change with temperature and as a scientist you know that!" he grinned, getting away from the point now.

"What is significant is that only a few weeks ago you told me and my mother the offer still stood. Has the temperature changed so much, Alex?"

"No wonder Bill called you The Terrier", he laughed. "Come on, let's get you back to the Sanctuary. I don't like the idea of your mother being on her own any longer than necessary".

Caroline felt he was patronising her. And no-one else had ever called her father Bill, as far as she knew. As they drew up outside the house, he referred again to the prowler.

"Whatever happens, don't ever come outside if there is someone about. 'Phone me. I'm only seconds away – well, minutes".

"Where do you live, Alex, or shouldn't I ask?"

"I'm your nearest neighbour, Caroline", he replied laconically.

"That accounts for a lot of things then," she said,

embarrassed not to have known before.

"Like what?" he asked huskily, slipping his arm around her shoulders and drawing her closer to him. Caroline didn't think she could endure the intimacy of his touch. Alarm bells began to ring a warning to her. Afraid to look at him, she said,

"It explains why your car was so close on a couple of occasions, for a start".

He inclined her head so she was forced to look at him and he gently brought his mouth down on hers. Her protests, if any, were silenced as the soft lips teased against hers for only a few moments.

For Caroline the sensation was deliciously thrilling.

"I was wondering if you'd realised it was me", he said thickly, drawing away from her slowly. "Yes, I've a confession to make, but it is to you and you alone. Promise?"

"Of course, if it's a confidence then it will remain so". Caroline said, welcoming the chance to push emotion down and try to gather control of her wayward feelings for the man she despised and desired.

"I'm on night duty on a regular basis for a while. Twice now, a prowler has been about – the one time I chased off up the village to try to head him off because the way he leaped over the fences on the other side of the road meant that he had to be heading for the back road to the village. Unfortunately he gave me the slip".

"Who was it?"

"I couldn't be sure. When I said at the restaurant that there is so much I could say, so much I daren't, I meant it. Trust me, Caroline".

"But what can I do?" she asked, avoiding promising trust to a man who could clearly have her eating from his palm if he dared to kiss her again like that.

"To be candid, the geese are a fine idea, but up to a point they impede me too! It means I have to observe from a greater distance. I'm afraid that if I should get too near they'll cackle anyway. Perhaps you ought to have trained them to listen to my footsteps!" he added light-heartedly.

She wondered whether she should tell him about seeing Hugh and Oliver Cory, and then thought better of it. She wanted to ask him so many questions but she still suspected him on certain things.

"Let's get you inside and see that your mother's okay. Hell, it's turned eleven, she'll probably be worrying and waiting", he added, looking at his watch. "Now, not a word to mum, okay? And I still think you're a lovely woman", he smiled, ducking playfully.

"Thanks for the lovely dinner, Alex, but you needn't have gone to such lengths to talk to me, you know".

"Och, woman, I'm trying to make amends and show you I'm a gentleman. I shall have to ask my friend Briggs to put in a wee word for me", he added lightly.

"He's done that already, I fear", Caroline said, letting herself in the front door.

Mrs Franklin was fast asleep in the lounge chair, the television playing to its disinterested audience. She woke with a start.

"Let me get you a coffee, Alex", she offered.

He declined, clearly anxious to be off.

Probably he wants to set himself to watch

somewhere, Caroline reflected.

As she saw him off at the door he said,

"By the way, if you should hear a horse – it'll be me. They're more effective chasing a prowler across country fields that a car ever could be. Now, be a good girl and get your beauty sleep".

He touched her affectionately on the nose with his forefinger, and then he was gone.

Sleep wouldn't come, however.

Caroline spent the first couple of hours tossing and turning, visualising Alex cantering about the countryside on horseback, chasing the nocturnal prowler. Could it be Oliver Cory? What had Hugh been handing him in Broadway? Was it pay-off money? Her mind boggled. It was too much like something out of an Agatha Christie novel. And yet, if it had been arson, if Oliver Cory had started the Cattery fire deliberately, then her father's death was murder. She got out of bed, hot and restless. The thought was positively frightening. No wonder Alex told her to be on her guard. He must suspect that such a thing could easily happen again.

Why wouldn't he declare his suspicions? What did he know that he wasn't prepared to admit? Surely he could and would trust Caroline? Why should he, though, she reflected. She didn't totally trust him either. She wanted to, she needed to, naturally. If only he would answer her questions honestly, frankly. He had said he wanted to put his cards on the table but he had definitely kept back all his trumps.

Caroline felt at a disadvantage.

Why was he prepared to go to all this trouble? What was he ultimately seeking?

Apart from a deliciously warm and tantalising goodnight kiss he had kept himself physically in check. But Caroline had sensed he was like a caged animal. A panther ready to pounce if given half a chance.

It was that half a chance which worried her. Throughout the evening she had been intensely aware of his maleness. His soft laughter had unnerved her and more than once he had looked at her with an implicit promise.

For her own part, her body had been far from indifferent to him. Chemical reactions are all very well and can be explained away quite logically in the science laboratory, she argued. How can you explain away the desire and need to be touched, caressed, held and loved by a man whom you have had every reason to loathe?

Where does trust come into the equation, she asked herself? For the answer was what she refused to accept. She wanted him to do all those things to her, and more. He stirred parts of her anatomy she had kept closed to anyone else, ever.

She had an infernal struggle going on inside her all evening and now the answer was written on her mind. She wanted him physically. She was ashamed to admit it to herself, but there it was.

The worse part of it was accepting that someone who could insult her, as he had done, could actually be desirable.

This was where her equation went wrong.

At some time in the early hours of the morning she had exhausted herself with unanswerable questions and some for which she knew the reply, but didn't approve.

As she fell into sleep she remembered John Gabriel saying, "Time is the devourer of things". Perhaps it would eat her problems away.

CHAPTER 6

It was nearly a month since she had been out for dinner with Alexander Sinclair and Caroline had been more than grateful for his non-appearance at the Sanctuary in all that time. Not that she didn't want to see him. Quite the contrary. But seeing him would completely destroy her resolve. Seeing him meant an awakening of all the female urges she had been desperately trying to drown from her conscious mind. Seeing him, being with him, meant the obvious corollary to Caroline, of wanting him.

A couple of months ago she would never have believed it possible that he could stir such feelings of longing and desire in her. It wasn't even as if there had been a great deal of physical contact.

After the first time, when he had called in the early hours, she had practically convinced herself that her feelings of need had been prompted by fear of the prowler, shock and cold. Hopefully too, that was all that Alex had concluded.

But the night of the meal in Stratford had proved to her beyond any doubt that he held a compelling physical attraction for her. He had the capability of drawing sexual urges from her simply by the look he gave, the inflection in his words, the tone in his voice. It was because it was so purely physical an attraction that Caroline was so afraid of it.

If he were to be aware of his attraction, of the feelings he was arousing in her…. the mere thought had terrified her during the last month.

She had trembled with the knowledge that he would be able to assert his power over her whenever he chose and she knew she would be unable to deny him. The idea of mere physical satisfaction had always repulsed her. The idea of sex without any other feelings of attachment, belonging and sharing, had been something she had always rejected.

Not that any male had ever before stirred her sufficiently to give the matter a second thought. Her work had always satisfied her and she had begun to come to the conclusion that 'that kind of thing' would pass her by. Her demands were too high.

Needless to say, even from University days she had endured the usual ribaldry and inferences to her 'spotless virginity' but it hadn't troubled her. She had placed a high value on her virginity. No green undergraduate could insult her into giving in to the purely physical. She always believed and wanted more from a relationship than a quick 'bed hop' with any Tom, Dick or Harry. She could not now imagine that it would be any more than just that with a man like Alex Sinclair. He had everything he wanted – position, money, charm, physical attraction. He could have his pick of attractive women. Dallying with the local female Vet, now that would be no more than a mere stimulation to his ego.

It would be quite an experience, though, Caroline contemplated, letting a man like Alex make love to you. Her thoughts began to curl around the fantasies which she visualised.

Holding onto the fantasy, bearing up to the reality and living with the future was more in keeping with her final thoughts on each occasion. And on this occasion she had plenty to occupy her mind, but there was a need to see Sinclair – if only to seek his advice. He had offered his help on many visits to the Sanctuary and Caroline had been reluctant to take him up on his offer. She felt she could cope, would cope, if he came near, so long as he didn't actually touch her in any way.

She simply had to get on with the fact of living with him nearby, and she must attempt to quell the physical need she had which he aroused in her. She could hardly really ignore him – after all, he was her nearest neighbour, a close friend to her mother and a professional colleague – even if he didn't quite see her in the same light regarding the latter category.

Caroline decided to get her mother to invite him over for a meal one evening. It would be by way of saying 'thank you' for his solicitous help regarding the prowler. Strange, she reflected, we've had no more bother on that score and even more, Sinclair has not been anywhere near for a month.

"Mr Sinclair said that they only got back last night", her mother was delighted to surprise Caroline with the news when later she did invite him for dinner.

"Back from where?" asked Caroline, trying to sound only vaguely interested, "and you said 'they'?"

"He did say where, dear, but I'm afraid I got a bit confused. Somewhere to do with Vet work. But it was a sort of holiday as well. Anyway, he took a young lady with him", she added "but I didn't like to ask questions, you know me, dear".

Panic bells rang in Caroline. Panic bells of jealousy. What right had she to be jealous, or even…? She wasn't involved with Sinclair. She had already decided that it would be a foolish course to run. On reflection it was just as well that she had made such a resolution, for clearly she was right and he appeared to have young women waiting at his elbow. The very last thing she must do would be to make a fool of herself.

Caroline was staggered with Alex Sinclair arrived for dinner with an attractive brunette on his arm.

"Mother", Caroline declared, exasperated as they watched their guests walk from the car. "What on earth possessed you to ask him to bring a guest? Under the circumstances, I think that's rather adding insult to injury", she pouted angrily.

"Under what circumstances?" her mother asked innocently.

"Oh, never mind", she was not intending to let her into any confidences if she could help it. "Who is she, anyway?" she demanded.

"I think we'll just have to wait and find out", Mrs Franklin said quite philosophically.

"Do you mean that he never said he was bringing a woman with him?"

"Oh yes", she said absentmindedly.

"You knew, but never said?" Caroline flung at her, feeling cheated.

"He asked me if he could bring a charming young lady with him. He said he thought we'd be pleased, as he certainly would".

"Then you'd better answer the door", she replied caustically to her mother as she flounced off upstairs on some pretext.

When she finally came back downstairs, they were all in conversation. Sinclair put his sherry glass on an adjacent coffee table and jumped up eagerly to introduce his lady friend.

"Caroline, it was a little presumption of me, I know, but your mother gave a seal of approval for me to bring a guest who's staying with me for a while."

"She hadn't warned me, if that's what you want to know", Caroline's voice was unsteady as she saw his eyes harden, but he ignored her rudeness and continued.

"Heather has accompanied me for the last couple of weeks at a seminar down in London. I thought it would be healthy for her to be involved in new surroundings for a while".

Heather, slender, attractive, a brunette looking slightly pale and timid, stood up and proffered her hand to Caroline.

"I'm delighted to meet you", her soft Scottish tone was gentle and sincere. "Alex has spoken very highly of you and what you are trying to achieve here".

Caroline reciprocated as warmly as she could but felt stabs of angered, jealous hurt inside her.

"You're very welcome", she lied, "pleased to meet you".

Alex had watched her carefully throughout and seemed well-pleased with the introduction.

"I desperately needed a partner for the two weeks in London, so Heather kindly filled the breach. A lot of it was tedious veterinary nonsense but most evenings the Society had lined up social functions – without a wife what can a man do but take along the next best thing".

Still standing, Alex slipped his arm around Heather and gave her a warm hug.

Caroline was wounded to the core. She'd seen that Conference advertised in her copy of their professional magazine but there had been little or no chance of her getting to it. Some of the lectures on offer during the second week had looked particularly appealing.

"Are you a Vet too, then?" Caroline tried desperately to sound curious and polite but hoped to stab Sinclair with some jibe later if Heather replied in the affirmative.

"Och, no!" Heather tried to cover an embarrassed smile, "I'm no' that clever, Miss Franklin. Besides I think one Vet in the family will be quite enough!"

The sting had all been to Caroline. She deserved the pain which Heather's answer gave to her and tried to cover it up by more questions if only to have Sinclair's steely impersonal stare taken off her.

"How on earth did you fill in the days then? Was it not a little boring waiting around for all those male Vets to get off their chauvinistic pedestals?" She should never have taken her jealousy out on Heather, and she regretted it immediately.

Heather had no idea what she was getting at and turned almost helplessly for defence to Alex.

"Caroline, Heather's not into all that chauvinism tosh which upsets you so much", he attempted light-heartedly to ease the tenseness of the situation but his look at Caroline held an implicit promise of retribution to come.

Mrs Franklin was not a mother for nothing and now realised what was upsetting her daughter.

She jumped to the rescue.

"Heather is Alex's sister, Caroline".

This embarrassment was all Caroline's and she murmured all the appropriate apologies. It was obvious though, even to Alex that she had completely misconstrued. What it had done, of course, was to reveal to Alex that Caroline's feelings towards him were more than surface deep. If anything by jumping to such conclusions, she had blown her chances of assuming to him that he meant nothing to her.

Over dinner Heather explained, somewhat haltingly and with emotion that she had not filled a breach for Alex, but it was rather the other way around. Harry, her husband of only two years, had been killed on active duty in Northern Ireland some months previously. She had lived with fear for his safety from the word go, but the loss was not easy to bear. It was Alex who had given her opportunity to take herself away from the distress.

"I knew that under the present circumstances you'd not be able to leave the Sanctuary – so I never broached the subject with you", Alex interjected, his eyes on Caroline with a thoughtful, narrowed gaze.
But it had crossed his mind, Caroline comforted herself inwardly.

"As a matter of fact Heather's to stay with me a wee while. I wondered if you'd be able to find her gainful employment for a while to keep her out of mischief?" He gave a wink of the conspirator to Mrs Franklin.

"I'd be able to help out with anything really", Heather said. I was a secretary in a law practice back in Edinburgh, actually, but I can turn my hand to anything", she offered willingly.

"Heather's left her job to be candid – it was my idea", Alex added honestly, "she'll be with me for a while until – well, until she's ready to do whatever she wants to do". He patted his sister's hand with such brotherly warmth and affection that Caroline felt little stabs of jealousy. Good heavens, she prodded herself, pull yourself together, it's his sister, not his mistress.

It gave Caroline a leading opportunity to talk to Alex about the granting of Charity status for the Sanctuary. Heather had had some experience of fundraising and there was no doubt that she would fit the bill as their Charity Fund Manager.

"She's a jolly good organiser, too", Alex added confidently, "that law practice in Edinburgh will fall apart without her. But that's their loss, eh, Heather?" It was settled. The timid, pale-looking Heather, suddenly alerted to a new interest in her life, became so animated and excited as all the discussion got under way over coffee. Papers were brought out, sketches, plans, ideas, suggestions, money raising ventures proposed. It was all written down carefully, in shorthand, by Heather.

"I'll have these notes copied up as our first record", she promised optimistically, "that is if I can have access to a machine".

"There's a computer at the practice in Broadway", Alex volunteered, "you can come in with me in the morning, if you like".

"Won't the girl be requiring to use it herself?" Heather queried, turning to her brother.

"Huh! That girl! Why ever Hugh appointed her, I'll never know. She's quite useless – can't type at all. Anyway, she's off sick according to the message

Hugh's left on my answerphone".

"If you're sure that I'll be no trouble – Alex – I know you from old. He's very bossy!" she added, turning to Caroline with a sly wink.

"You don't say!" Caroline feigned surprise. "Incidentally", she asked, "How is Hugh, Alex? We've not seen nor heard from him for weeks".

"Oh", Alex registered obvious surprise at Caroline's sudden interest in his partner, "don't you and he keep in regular contact?" There was a tightening in his voice and posture.
Caroline tried hurriedly to think of a quick retort, but only mumbled,

"Well, normally he … that is, it's unusual … after all, he was paying weekly visits here at one time".

"You told me you'd put a stop to anyone visiting the Sanctuary", Alex cut in curtly.

"You still call, though", Mrs Franklin added gently.

"Ah, but my visits are purely personal and friendly and they're certainly not chargeable!"

If Caroline had hoped to get information from Alex, she had failed. He looked at her harshly and she felt decidedly miserable. He countered her attacks every time. It left her feeling stupid and wanting to loathe him. Heather's timely visit to the Sanctuary had been most fortuitous for Caroline.

Within a week Heather had rearranged Mr Franklin's old office, something which Caroline had found it hard to bring herself to do. She set up an excellent filing system, produced masses of lists of people to contact, important names to invite to functions, schools to advise and visit for fundraising, firms to ask for financial help, samples, sponsorship and so on. Caroline had no doubt that Alex's sister was the kind of manager they required to get the Sanctuary back on its feet. She admitted, very readily to herself that she was a good Vet, but administration was better left to the likes of Heather. A good organiser, a keen worker and an enthusiastic supporter. What more could they ask for?

Caroline never regretted for a moment that they had taken her on. It left Caroline with a lot more opportunity to deal with the practical side of the Sanctuary. Unfortunately, it also gave her far too much time to think about Alex. He was still keeping his distance, dropping Heather off in the mornings at the Sanctuary, never lingering except to chat with Mrs Franklin. Caroline was usually dashing off to Cheltenham anyway and by the time she got back most evenings, Heather had gone back to Alex's home. Always there would be a very neatly typed-up report of all Heather's activities, 'phone calls, jobs she had dealt with, jobs she intended to carry out. Caroline was delighted with the progress. Money had actually been donated, bank accounts looked much healthier – so much that she couldn't possibly have achieved on her own.

Alex had somehow managed to wheedle the computer out of the office at Broadway for the first few weeks, but now Heather was hoping to organise their own equipment. The question of wages for Heather had originally been put on one side when in fact she agreed to work for nothing until she proved her worth.

Being out in Cheltenham all week, it was really only at the weekends that she had much opportunity, if at all, to see Alex. She couldn't come to terms with her desire for him on the one hand, and her own rejection of him on the other. She had not been able to quell the intoxicating, heady desires she felt and had tried so hard to suppress. She was so muddled up emotionally. She suspected he had plenty of liaisons to keep his libidinous desires satisfied and she resented her own feelings of need for him all the more because of it.

She did not want to cheapen herself by any hint or display to him and the battle was always there to subjugate such feelings of passion and arousal which stirred in her whenever she so much as saw him. To give way to those emotions would have destroyed her own self-esteem and her position with him. It was still better for her to practise a hostile approach to warn him off. She had no desire to be simply one of his conquests, just someone he could take out if he felt bored or ... the thought overwhelmed her. Someone obviously did enjoy pleasures with him.

A healthy male of his attraction and charm would hardly be able to curb a naturally hungry sexual appetite.

She had tried, once in a while, to pick up any kind of hint from Heather but the latter either knew nothing or was discreet enough not to discuss her brother with her in that way.

One evening in late July Alex invited Caroline and her mother to a 'progress dinner' at his home.

In all the time the Franklins had owned the Sanctuary, Caroline had never seen Alex's house. It was more than a surprise, therefore, when she drove to dinner on the Saturday evening.

The house was extremely well-set back from the

main road and was approached along a tree-lined drive. Caroline was fairly stunned. Cleeve Court was a substantial Regency house built of stone, set on a rise at the end of the drive. It looked solid, imposing and very superior.

"Oh mother", she declared in gawping wonder, "does Alex Sinclair actually own this? What on earth did he want with our humble Animal Sanctuary and our few measly acres?"

"Why don't you ask him?" came the non-committal reply.

Caroline felt the timing of such a question now would be inappropriate.

In front of the house there were paddocks and she recognised immediately the black stallion Alex had ridden across their land one morning. She reddened now, remembering how rudely she had rebuked him and how embarrassed she had been at his retort. Her father would have been ashamed of her – she knew that. But there had been so much else which she hadn't known.

She still didn't feel in control of this situation. Her reactions to Alex Sinclair were motivated now by her instinctive desire for self-preservation against his intense maleness and the sexual power he had which she was so afraid of.

At the entrance porch she tugged at an ancient bell pull which responded with a clanging, deafening ring that must have echoed up the whole valley. A huge, heavy timbered front door, set in a doorway of intricately carved stonework, was opened by a large, rosy-cheeked woman of ample proportions.

"Mr Sinclair's been called out on a 'mergency, I 'spect 'e'll be back shortly. Come in do, my dears.

'Ello again, my dear, 'ow's yourself?" she looked directly at Mrs Franklin and slipped her arm through hers and proceeded to lead the way into the Drawing Room.

"Not too bad, Mrs B, we're keeping ourselves pretty busy now Heather's involved with us. She's a proper little worker", Caroline's mother responded.

"They're all the same, these Sinclairs. Still, at least they work for it – not like some folks – get it landed on a plate and then 'buse it something criminal. I'll leave you in 'ere a while, my dears 'cos I've food to tend to in the kitchen".

Heather walked in at that point.

"Och, how lovely you look, Caroline", she beamed.

The silky black dress had been chosen specially, although she didn't want to admit it. In Cheltenham during a quiet break after surgery in the week, she had slipped into Curtis's, renowned for its prices but exclusivity. If the dress had attracted his sister's eye, there would be no saying what it might do to Alex. The bodice clung to her breasts and plunged low, even lower at the back, and flowed into a swinging, swirling skirt. It was so soft she hardly felt that she was wearing it.

A small silver pendant fell tantalisingly to her cleavage.

"I'm sorry Alex had to rush off a couple of hours ago. Hugh Morrison was supposed to be on call this weekend, but Alex said he's nowhere to be found".

"What's the problem?"

"Och, you know Alex, Caroline. He didn' say where, when or what. He puts on his Vet's hat and cloak when he leaves the drive. He's always been the same. You could never get him to discuss work at home".

"A good policy to adopt – very strong-minded!" Caroline agreed.

"Would you like me to show you a bit of the house while we're waiting for Alex? – I'm sure he'll not mind".

"It seems a little presumptuous", Caroline demurred, but was longing to see Alex's home.

"I'll just wait here for you, if you don't mind, Heather – I've seen around before", Caroline's mother replied, taking a seat in the window. Caroline's surprise was registered, but she said nothing, not wishing to appear foolish in front of Heather.

It seemed that her mother had kept her in the dark on rather a lot of issues. It occurred to her then that on arriving, Mrs B, the housekeeper, had treated her mother like an old friend.

Heather took her into the Library and Caroline could picture Alex dominating from the massive oak desk set in the stone mullioned bay window. The view was across a delightful area of sweeping lawns and flower beds. Beyond this was an expanse of rhododendron, no longer in bloom, but Caroline could visualise the scene in Spring.

"There's a lovely paved lavender walk beyond the steps leading up to the orchard", Heather pointed out.

"And a lily pond with a shrubbery and a multitude of shrubs and trees!"

Alex's voice startled them both.

"Did you not show Caroline the grounds yet?" he asked Heather. "Never mind, I'll show you after dinner. Sorry I was not here when you arrived", he apologised, smiling broadly.

"I never heard your car", Heather said.

"Because I went on the original horse power!" he re-joined. "'Twas a field job after all!"

Caroline trembled, suppressing the desires that invaded her. The way he was looking at her made her catch at her breath as she quelled the shivering sensation which teased at her. He stood, legs slightly astride, dressed in black riding boots and cavalry twill trousers. His shirt of country check was opened at the neck. She gasped inwardly. He was devastatingly attractive to her, even dressed so casually. Her adrenalin was flowing as she knew he could read her senses. His eyes were reluctant to leave her and she swallowed dryly in desperation.

"Is everything … is … I mean, is everything in hand now, Alex?" she stuttered nervously.

"Oh, I think so. Yes, I think everything's fine". There was an enigmatic gleam in his eyes as his interest rested ruthlessly on the full curves of her black bodice. His teeth glinted, devilishly white against the tan of his face.

"Let Mrs B know I'm back will you, and there's sherry in the Drawing Room, if you'd be so kind, Heather?"

His slight hesitation caused Caroline to flutter weakly.

"I'll shower and be with you in no time", he said, slowly drawing his eyes to meet Caroline's. There was something deliberate in his hint of showering and Caroline found herself tortured with the thought of his naked body. She gave him a helpless glance as he turned on his heel and left the Library.

He knew!

What a little idiot she was to think she could disarm him and get away with it. He had only to look at her in this helpless state and he had triumphed. How inexperienced I am, she admitted to herself. Never having been in this position before, she scarcely knew how to combat it with equanimity. She had never been to lectures that covered such elemental topics as the force of feelings she experienced now.

Perhaps it would not be so difficult if she could be sure that the outcome of a relationship with him would not be what she had so far feared. He could and probably would use her to amuse himself.

That was why the battle raged within her so furiously. If only she could yield to her emotions freely and confidently and experience the sincere and honest response she felt ought to be a natural outcome.

Sitting in the window seat in the Drawing Room, she could see the gateway set in the stone wall which Heather had said led to a walled kitchen garden where there were greenhouses.

"Do you … does Alex have a gardener?" she asked naively.

"Och, yes, there's too much for him to take on here. Anyway, he's not really a green fingers type you know, so don't let him mislead you. Mrs B's husband is the Chief Gardener".

"What's Mr B's name?" Caroline queried, trying to steady her voice as the mere thought of being misled by Alex thrilled her to the core.

"Their surname's Maxwell really – he's Isaac. They only call her Mrs B – it's a name that stuck from Uncle Angus's day. B is for Boss!"

Caroline was bemused.

"Uncle Angus said she was the Boss – without her, nobody could go about the daily business. 'Good food and a good roof and domestic care are of paramount importance', he used to say. Alex couldn't call her anything else".

Later Caroline found out how Mrs B had earned her reputation. She had prepared a meal 'par excellence'.

Caroline felt she had truly had a gastronomic journey. For starters there had been an hors d'oeuvre of shellfish with cold entrées. This was followed by a white fish with white meat, sauce and vegetables, then pheasant in a brown sauce. To follow, there was a variety of French cheeses and fresh fruit.

Alex had opened a bottle of Chardonnay and toasted the success of the Sanctuary.

Over dinner he explained how he had come into possession of Cleeve Court, which had been built in the early nineteenth century for a clerical gentleman. Angus Sinclair, Alex's uncle, who was knighted in the early sixties, had come into ownership in the early fifties.

"I don't approve of how he made his money, mind", Alex was quick to point out, "he was Chairman of a tobacco company. Even his wife died from smoking the damned things. She unfortunately left him childless".

"And that's where you came in?" Caroline suggested.

"Not quite that easy, I'm afraid", he cut in with acid denunciation.

"There was a dispute over the will", Heather informed.

"I'd spent a lot of my boyhood years here. Uncle Angus was a past master at making a young lad feel life was one big adventure. He taught me to ride. My black stallion was his gift to me on graduation. It was hard for him not being able to share his life with sons. Aye", he sat back reflecting, "he was a grand old man, and I loved him dearly".

"But why should the will be contested?" Caroline queried.

"Brothers. Brothers with greedy hands", he replied sardonically.

"Whose? Yours?" Caroline had little enough idea of Alex's background. He steadied his gaze and asked tersely.

"Have you any idea just how much this lot is worth?"
She shook her head numbly.

"Well ..." he hesitated. "Needless to say when Uncle Angus left it with me as sole beneficiary there was a bit of a ding dong, eh, Heather?" he sought his sister's agreement.

"Come on little Caroline, don't look so stunned – I'll show you around the grounds".

Before she knew what had hit her they were both outside in the cobbled courtyards.

"And that's the squash court to the left of the stable block", he pointed out, slipping his left arm under her right elbow to steady her. "If you'd not got your posh shoes on I'd walk you across all the woodland. Some of the original trees of Oak, Ash and Beech still remain but there was a lot of planting done in the fifties. Now it's even more varied from

Scots Pine and Lawsons Cypress to Sycamore and Larch".

"It sounds wonderful", she replied cheerfully.

"I plan to dedicate it to the Forestry Commission eventually". His arm slid possessively around her waist.

She wanted to protest but couldn't.

"Come, I'll show you the Lavender Walk. The fragrance there mingled at this time of evening with honeysuckle will send you dizzy", he promised.

Caroline couldn't tell him that she felt quite dizzy enough already.

Out of sight of the house, through shrubbery beyond a small lily pond, he pulled her into him. The male scent of him invaded her nostrils and her heart began to beat unevenly.

"Caroline".

His voice, the soft Scottish burr, caused her to catch her breath.

His eyes were dark and intense and a shiver of sensation gripped her body. He bent his head towards her and her eyes closed as his mouth touched hers. She trembled, suppressing a desire to curl her fingers around the back of his neck and pull his mouth down more firmly.

A strange, ineffable warmth invaded her body as he slowly, softly explored her mouth. His voice was murmuring her name, gently, caressingly and the tiny vibrations caused tingling in her lips. Her mouth had gone very dry, her body was becoming hotter as she felt the penetration of his tongue as it stroked firmly inside her mouth. Her arms wound around him.

His one hand slipped down to her hips and in one fierce movement he pulled her in closer to him and she felt his own hot arousal as she pressed herself willingly into him.

"Oh, Alex", she moaned.

Huskily he whispered against her ear as she experienced the thrilling heat of his arousal when their hips seemed to rotate with the passion that gripped them both.

"I want you, Caroline", he purred.

She had jettisoned caution and self-preservation. Murmurings of pleasure in her throat urged him on. He slipped his hand into the front of her bodice and groaned with delight as he felt the hardened bud of her nipple, played with it between finger and thumb while his mouth bore voraciously on hers.

"God, I want you", he murmured again, "I want to feel your skin against mine". His dark head bent over to her breast as he eased it from her bodice, his mouth brushing sensitively across the nipple bringing a small moan of delight from her. She gripped him to her as his hand slid to the other breast and he repeated the tracing of his mouth across the nipple, hard and prominent.

His lips came back to hers, possessive and demanding, claiming.

Her hands were inside his jacket, pressed against the hardness of his chest as she felt the heat burning through his shirt. Without realising what she was doing, she unbuttoned his shirt and shuddered with the heated erotic contact of her bared breasts against his chest. An upsurge of desire forced a more passionate and husky demand from him.

"Caroline, let me make love to you. I've wanted to touch you all night. I must have you", his muscles were straining, his skin was hot and damp.

She heard herself moan his name.

"Yes, Alex, yes, oh please", and she felt the answering pressure of his body against her and then his mouth over her breast making her shudder with paroxysms of pleasure so intense that she became aware of wanting to faint with weakness.

Suddenly, from across the orchard came the screeching of a magpie whose raucous sound cut through their passion.

Alex tensed and slowly pulled away from her with reluctance, apologising hoarsely,

"I'm sorry Caroline – I've … I'm so sorry, I completely lost control of myself, I …" he began buttoning his shirt.

Caroline was in a state of shock. A sob threatened to choke her. She suddenly went cold from shame and embarrassment.

"It's not your fault, I … I'm, it was … I'm sorry too. Whatever must you think of me?"

She awkwardly tried to adjust her dress and felt disgusted with herself pushing the hot, swollen breast back into the clammy bodice of her dress as he turned respectfully away.

"Caroline, look, I'm truly sorry. It was damned indecent and an utterly reprehensible thing for me to do. Quite unforgivable. Whatever does the word hospitality mean?" he tried to laugh self-consciously. "I'm sorry, really – I promise I never invited you over to dinner to seduce you in the shrubbery. Well, I mean, that's not …"

"I think I know quite what you mean", Caroline averred, hotly embarrassed with shame and degradation at her own part in the incident.

"Look, I don't want you to think …" he began.

"But Caroline – that dress, your perfume – I confess, I simply lost control. It's so unlike me. God! He ran his fingers through his hair. "Whatever must you think of me?"

"Thinking is the last thing I'll be doing, Alex", she said stoutly and started to walk hurriedly back through the Lavender Walk.

She had let herself go completely. It was her own fault entirely for dressing so wantonly and being so shameless in her acceptance of what she had allowed him to do to her.

"You carry on indoors", he called softly after her, "I'll just put the horses in for the night".

Caroline was glad of his excuse. It gave her the opportunity to try and compose herself, but she felt that Heather could sense what might have happened in the shrubbery.

CHAPTER 7

The rest of the evening for Caroline was fraught with tenseness. She could scarcely look at Alex for it immediately resurrected the passion and emotion experienced in the shrubbery earlier. That made her worse, because in the first place she had been so embroiled in it, so responsible for it and had found it so pleasurable. In the second place she was suffering from acute embarrassment knowing that Alex had found her so easy, so wanton, so willing. And he had taken every advantage of the situation. She felt she had thoroughly degraded and cheapened herself. Still she could feel his hands, his lips, his body. The sensations had been so overwhelming.

Never had she experienced such rousing passion. Her body had never been teased into such wild ecstatic responses. Her mind had told her she was wanton but her body had been unable to display any modesty as a searing desire had consumed her. She had throbbed with aching yearning for a man whom she had loathed and now she wanted him to make violent love to her.

Gone was her tight control. Evaporated was her stern resolve. Shattered was her self-respect while she sat in the same room, knowing that his husky groans had allowed him whatever licence he desired, for she had proved herself incapable of resisting. The violence of her own response appalled her. She should never allow him to get that close again. Even as she let the thought pass through her mind she knew she had already tried before to make the same resolve. This time, she promised herself, it would be different.

After all, she had hardly expected that he would attempt to ravage her in the shrubbery. Her mother and his sister might have come out at any moment to join them.

How could she stop him from taking such a liberty with her again? Why should she? The moral side of her knew the answer to that. But the renegade spirit kept whispering to her that she didn't want to stop Alex. After all, he hadn't been entirely to blame. She had scarcely resisted his advance, more to the point, she had urged him on by her positive response to his fervour.

She wanted to feel what it was like to sate herself in his passion. She longed to unbridle all her own repressed and smothered ardour. He had kindled a fire and she wanted secretly to fan the flames. She ached to have him assuage the long pent-up emotions she had scarcely known had been within her. Perhaps it was too late now. They do say that what you haven't had, you never miss. But Alex had stirred her body. Now she wanted more than anything to indulge herself in feelings of such intensity that they raged within her, forcing all other logical thoughts to the back of her mind.

This is insanity, she told herself, stealing a look at him, only to be caught doing so by Alex himself. His eyes were reluctant to leave and he raised his eyebrows in a hint of intimacy between them.

She breathed in, quickly, deeply.

A lot of talking had been going on around her. She had given the appearance of being involved, but most of it had passed her by as she fantasised in intoxicating, reckless thoughts of wild lovemaking in the arms of a man whom up to now she had despised.

"Are you with us then, Caroline?" Alex's voice came across a chasm of mere feet to interrupt her reverie.

"Yes, I beg your pardon … I was miles away for a moment …," she apologised, reddening.

"Where are you?" his soft Scottish voice whispered only to her. He had come across to take her empty glass. "Can I give you another glass of wine, Caroline?" And as his hand took the glass from her his fingers touched hers gently, fleetingly but purposely. "Where were you?" he murmured even more softly, "as if I couldn't guess".

"I think perhaps no more wine, thank you Alex", she smiled shakily, "the journey home is only short, but a car drive nevertheless".

"Och, I'll not hear of you driving back – I'll be taking you both, then we can get your car back tomorrow", he insisted.

"Certainly not, there's no need, really …" she vainly protested.

"I'll hear no more of it, Caroline", he asserted firmly, "besides, it will be dark – I'll just make sure of your safety and so forth".

It was useless to object further, particularly as her mother had already murmured agreement.

"Now, what do you think of Heather's idea of an Open Day – to boost your funds, supporters, sponsors, improve the publicity and so on?"

"I think it's a wonderful idea. But can you cope?" she appealed to Heather across the room, "you've already a great deal on your timetable".

"Och, I've no doubts about my coping, Caroline", she reassured, "it's just what I'd revel in. I'd love to take the reins on a venture like this".

"See", said Alex, handing another glass of wine to Caroline, having quite ignored her protest, "Heather's already halfway there. There's no stopping a Sinclair, you know, when they're on a mission!"

There was an ominous ring to his voice and more than an enigmatic gleam in his eye. Caroline sensed he was no longer talking about Heather and Sanctuary Open Day!

It occurred to her that he displayed alarming zeal in his intent on the success of the Sanctuary. Only a few months ago he had wanted to buy it. She had never solicited his reasons from him.

"Who would want to stop a Sinclair? Who dare?" she proffered light-heartedly.

"Exactly!" he replied, a cynical twist of the lips given as an excuse for a smile.

Caroline looked at him and half drowned in the depth of his eyes. Just looking at Alex caused such a stir in her sea of emotions that simply to stay afloat with normality was difficult.

Caroline recognised that if Heather had not appeared then her relationship with Alex Sinclair would never have become such a dilemma to her. As it was, Heather's efficiency and competence at running the Sanctuary had led to Caroline's inordinate amount of freedom.

Freedom from work, responsibility and time-consuming, all-absorbing days and evenings. It had also brought her into constant contact with Alex now that he had, through Heather, more of a foothold in the Sanctuary.

"Right ladies", Alex said decisively, "then tomorrow being Sunday, we'll spend the day in organising. In the meantime I'll take the guests home".

All the security lights were on as Caroline had suggested to the girls at the kennels and two of the volunteer dog walkers had stayed behind to help keep an eye on things.

Whether it was the wine or just the way Alex had pecked her, ever so slightly, on the cheek, in front of her mother, Caroline couldn't tell. She went to bed in a haze, half smothering Whistler with warmth and emotion that quite possibly was really meant for a human recipient!

Caroline had gone through some kind of metamorphosis. Nothing would ever be the same again. Nothing could ever be the same again. Since Alex had taken her out to dinner she had vacillated between desire and hate, half-believing that the latter would expunge the ardour and need she felt for him. But it was too late. The devastation to her emotions had taken place. No man had ever stirred her at all. Perhaps that was why she had pursued a relentless academic course for so long. Or was it because of it? She had never known anything else.

Whatever had stirred her now, and that would be a query to answer sooner rather than later, had caused her to question what had motivated her for so many years.

Now she had reached her objective. She had it all. Or did she? Caroline knew now there was something missing. It had taken a long time to manifest itself but the arousals within her pointed to her need for physical love. The masterly display from Alex in the shrubbery had testified to that without a doubt.

How though, could she allow herself to indulge in physical love with a man whom she thought she loathed? How could the two ideas be married together? Wouldn't it simply be a disgusting act of self-indulgence to enjoy the excesses of sexual gratification? Could it be possible to indulge in sexual gratification with a man if you disliked him so? Where was the honesty and the propriety in doing such a thing? Could she, in truth, fling herself with honesty into his arms?

What choice did she have? She demanded of herself. How could she carry on from day to day, curbing emotions like this when Alex knew she wanted him physically and there seemed little point in trying to pretend otherwise? If that is all that it is, she reasoned, it would be better to let the emotions have their rein. Why not follow it through and experience the full intimacy of him? All things should be tested, experiments followed, conclusions drawn from results.

That was what her training had been all about, surely? But then in all that time she had no recourse to test herself in this way. Always her own conscious judgement had been enough, she reasoned. All that reasoning; all that sensible wisdom; all that sound exposition was meaningless in this situation. Letting the experience take its course should be easy enough, she calculated coldly, mentally, as her skin shivered with excitement at the mere thought of what could be enacted. The results would be difficult to admit. There was no question in Caroline's mind she would enjoy the experience.

The problem would be in accepting that it might be a 'one-off'. Suppose that Alex Sinclair thrilled her so much she wanted more and he would or could not assuage her ardour? Suppose he chose to use her, to abuse her? What if he was imprudent and perverse in his attitude afterwards?

As it stood, Caroline was devastated by the desire to have him make love to her. It would have to be so. No more resolve. No more repressed emotions. No more resistance to her body's crying need.

Caroline had no idea what time it was when sleep finally overtook her exhausted mind and body.

Sunday should have been a calm day of rest and relaxation but it had been planned otherwise.

The volunteer staff had started arriving early, and after a quick breakfast Caroline, shrugging off her mother's solicitude for her state of health and her tired looks, went off to the kennels to check on a whelping bitch.

How could she tell her mother that a sleepless night had resulted in her decision to let the local Vet make love to her at the earliest opportunity? In the cold light of day the thought sounded ludicrous and distasteful.

Heather arrived driving Caroline's car and Alex was close behind as Caroline came across the gravel from the kennels.

Her mouth went dry. Pull yourself together, Caroline, she told herself as she felt herself going weak and dizzy like a silly teenager. Alex moved towards her purposefully. His shirt was opened revealing fully the curls of dark hair on his broad chest, his tight fitting trousers hugged his lean hips which seemed to be flaunting themselves with legs long and strong as he strode right to her.

"I shan't be able to stop, Caroline, I'm sorry. Heather's got all my ideas on paper".

There was more than a trace of irritation in his voice and she stiffened instinctively at the hardness of his expression. No explanation was forthcoming about his complete reversal of manner towards her.

"I'll be back later on today for Heather but she could walk up the lane anyway, if I'm delayed", he said tersely.

"Have you got to work after all?" she asked, trying not to reveal her intense disappointment at not having him around her as she had hoped.

"You could say that", he replied with acid denunciation. "Give my apologies to your mother, I really do have to dash off now", he flung over his shoulder.

Caroline felt devastated.

What had happened since last night? Perhaps Heather might be able to throw some light on her brother's change of attitude. She wouldn't be able to ask her directly, of course, but maybe…in a roundabout way.

Heather had gone straight into her office and was already busy at the computer. Caroline tried to appear casual, but inside her stomach felt as if it had turned upside down.

"Alex said you'd some notes on his ideas?" she asked.

"Oh, yes, he's done them hurriedly – I'm afraid they're still in my shorthand – I'm just typing them back for you now".

"Right, I'll pop back later then. Alex seemed … he's had to dash off, I gather?" Could Heather detect the real reason Caroline was asking, she wondered?

"It's since Hugh Morrison came. It's clean upset Alex this morning".

"Hugh? What did he want?" she asked without thinking. Of course, she had no right to ask such personal questions.

"I'm afraid I don't know, Caroline, but it really got to Alex. I hope he's not upset you. I can accept his not being civil to me, I'm just his sister and at least I've had years of understanding him. When something gets to Alex like that, though, it's got to be very serious. He was even rude to Mrs B!"

"Oh dear", Caroline murmured sympathetically, "and you've no idea … what time did Hugh come then?"

"It must have been straight after breakfast because he was fine until then".

"Was he expecting Hugh?" Caroline persisted.

"I'm sorry, Caroline", Heather apologised, "honestly, I really don't know. If I did know, of course, I'd tell you. But don't worry, he'll get over it – he's not one to be upset for long is Alex", she reassured.

For the rest of the day Caroline found it very hard to put her mind on anything. Just the fact that he wasn't around when she had expected him to be was enough to disturb her composure. The fact that something to do with Hugh Morrison had caused a complete change of attitude in Alex worried her and enabled her to put all manner of interpretations into the situation. Significantly, Hugh had kept an exceedingly low profile for weeks. She had been relieved, of course, not to have to fend off his unwelcome attentions. Since she had seen him that day in Broadway giving Oliver Cory an envelope, she had had hesitations about trusting him at all. Now she was filled with apprehension over this new turn of events.

Oliver Cory had a cloud of suspicion hanging over him as far as Caroline was concerned. She had managed to get her mother to remember that Hugh had sent Oliver Cory to offer himself for work with her father. He had suggested him – recommended him, in fact, her mother recalled.

Caroline knew it would, under normal circumstances, be wrong to put any false interpretation into the situation. But since the fire, Oliver Cory had not appeared. He had not come to her father's funeral. Then she had seen him with Hugh in what looked to her like rather compromising circumstances.

Hugh had kept his distance and his seemingly relentless pursuit of Caroline appeared to have cooled off.

Then there was the question of his offer for the Sanctuary. He had never even mentioned it to Caroline. She still didn't even know if he'd mentioned it to his partner, Alex.

Alex.

Every time she came to a halt that day it was thinking about Alex! Just when she had made a decision to let her emotions have full rein with him, he had given her the cold shoulder.

Much to her mother's chagrin, she was unable to eat lunch.

"I think you're sickening for something, dear", she had said, concerned.

Caroline would like to have agreed with her but spent the next couple of hours trying to get to grips with all the arrangements for the Open Day with Heather.

By five o'clock Alex had not reappeared so Caroline offered to drop his sister back at Cleeve Court. She wished her motive had been purely altruistic but secretly hoped that there might be an opportunity to see if Alex had returned home.

She spent the evening proof reading the Sanctuary Newsletter and adding a couple of items for Heather to include on the final sheet on Monday.

The Newsletter had been Caroline's idea to get information to all the supporters. Heather had initiated a membership society called simply The Friends of Franklin Sanctuary. For a nominal amount a supporter became a member of the supporter's club, received a badge and a monthly newsletter. The costs were kept as low as possible but Heather had suggested sponsorship each month by a local business and had gone to the trouble of getting a dozen or more willing people to do just that. It meant that one business would only have to 'cough up' their costs for advertising on the back of the Newsletter once in each year but would actually get twelve months coverage.

Alex had agreed, as a partner, to let Broadway Veterinary Practice be one of their sponsors. It was good for the Sanctuary, he said, to have the professional backing and at the same time good enough for Hugh and himself, to encourage more business for themselves.

Heather had been responsible for a complete upsurge in the fortunes of the Sanctuary. There had, because of her unstinting efforts, been a new wave of help.

"Once generated, Caroline, you have to keep it on the boil", Heather had urged early on.

How right she had been. She had left nothing to chance. She even had the bright idea of making a video of the Sanctuary and its work to take round to schools, clubs and other organisations.

Caroline had planned to take her mother, the following day, down to her sister's home in Cornwall for a short holiday. She had arranged with Mr Avery Briggs to have a few days off. At the back of her mind had been the half hope that Alex might even offer or suggest to go but…Monday came too soon and still there was no indication or hint that Alex might come to see her mother off. Caroline deliberately procrastinated hoping against hope that he would put his apparent anger on one side and call to see her mother.

By mid-morning her mother was getting edgy to go. It had been arranged that she would stay herself one night at her aunt's house to avoid the long journey back on the same day.

Caroline would never, under normal circumstances have done such a thing, but she used Heather as an excuse to call at Cleeve Court. Under normal arrangements Heather would have been at the Sanctuary long before Caroline left for Cornwall, but because of all the work she had put in on the Sunday, it had been agreed that she would take the morning off.

"I'll drop the proof-reading in to Heather – there's just a couple of points I want to make sure she's aware of", Caroline excused herself to her mother.

"Won't she be coming round later anyway, dear?" her mother queried.

"Well, I'll drop this off now", she said, a slight embarrassment lest her mother should be able to read her thoughts and actions too clearly.

But all the subterfuge was to no avail. When she pulled up at Cleeve Court, Mrs B informed her that Heather was out and that Mr Sinclair had not returned home since the previous morning.

In such an unhappy state of desolation, Caroline drove her mother to Cornwall. It was the unhappiest journey she had ever made.

They stopped for a light lunch but Caroline could scarcely swallow a morsel for the ache in her was so intense. All she could think about was Alex. She wanted to cry with longing that gnawed at her and the hardest part of the day was trying not to let her mother suspect that anything was wrong.

Her aunt's property was set back in about six acres, high on the coast road between Penzance and Helston. It overlooked countryside and sea and seemed to offer the best of both worlds. Her aunt used part of the land as a small Caravan and Camping site during the season.

The rest of the land was cleverly separated into sections, each sheltered by a belt of trees and high Escallonia hedges to protect her market garden plots from the ravages of winter winds that blew in mercilessly from the sea.

She cultivated Kaffir Lilies, Christmas trees and

any other crop she took her mind to. She never made a fortune, she said, "but I'm happy, I'm free and I owe nobody nothin', my dear".

Taking leave of them next morning, Caroline felt an unnatural eagerness to be on her way. Normally she welcomed staying at Tregonna House, as her mother couldn't help remarking when she kissed her goodbye.

"It'll all work out Cal, dear", her mother hugged her knowingly.

Caroline felt a lump in her throat and couldn't bring herself to reply. She only felt the more guilty at her anxiety to leave people she loved deeply to rush back to an uncertain reception with a man she scarcely dared to trust her feelings with.

Apart from stopping for coffee and petrol, Caroline drove all the way non-stop. She knew that her mind was not fully on the road.

It was hard not to be pressing every mile to go more quickly. She was filled with uncertainty and torment. She would be relying now on Alex to make the necessary overtures towards her. She would put herself in his way as much as she could and, without making it too obvious, give him the opportunity to seduce her.

The mere thought that he might no longer wish to seduce her had crossed her mind. His behaviour towards her on Sunday morning gave every indication that his ardour had cooled dramatically.

She had to believe that that was a temporary set-back. He must still surely want to make love to her as he had begged in the shrubbery? As to what would happen after that, Caroline, normally so far-seeing and prudent, had not given too much thought.

She saw the whole thing in its first stage as a very necessary exercise and an experiment. How could she know with any certainty what would ensue?

She didn't even know if what she felt was simple lusting, a craving to satisfy bodily needs she knew she had never experienced before. She only knew now that she was consumed with a desire for her body to experience to the full what only Alex had shown her was possible. How could she know the outcome?

Was it by any chance that she loved Alex? Is that what these feelings were?

For the last thirty miles or so Caroline found it difficult to register on anything. If she didn't get home soon she would be a danger to other road users. She was agitated, expectant and afraid as she drew into the drive.

The worst was to come.

Hugh Morrison's car was parked outside the house and he was just walking to his car carrying the computer.

It was obvious that explanations were in order. Heather was standing, hands on hips, in the doorway.

"What's going on?" she called out, diving out of her car.

"I'm taking back my equipment, Caroline", he shouted petulantly.

"But I thought… I thought you had loaned it to us…"

"Sinclair wheeled it out of the office, if that's what you mean", he shouted angrily, slamming down the boot of his car.

"But I thought that Alex said…" she began.

"Oh, it's Alex now, alright, isn't it?" he sneered, grabbing her wrists and shouting fiercely at her. "You bloody little tart, you've been playing quite a little game, haven't you?" he stormed.

"Whatever's got into you Hugh, let me go immediately", she cried.

"Let you go… huh! I've no intention of letting you go, Caroline, but until you fix up a date and set our relationship right, I'm giving nothing away, do you hear?"

"What are you talking about? What date? It's only in your head, not in mine, Hugh Morrison. I've never given you a hint of my intentions on that issue. You and I have just been friends. Anything more is just your fancy".

Caroline tried to wriggle free from his grip.

"You've been playing fast and loose with me, you damned little…damn you…"

"Hugh, now just you let me go before I ask Heather to set the geese on you," Caroline demanded.

"You haven't heard the last of this, Cal, I warn you", he threatened. Caroline was shaking with fury as Hugh screeched out of the drive.

Heather ran to her.

"Oh Caroline, I couldn't stop him. It's his machine right enough, isn't it? Och, come on inside and let me get you a strong drink – you're shaking all over, and is it any wonder with that man behaving like a lunatic?"

It was all too much. Caroline burst into tears as all the pent up emotions of the last few days overwhelmed her. Tears of anger, hurt and need all raged like a swollen torrent.

"I'm sorry you had to hear all that, Heather", she sobbed, after a while. "I can't think what's got into Hugh Morrison".

"He's a jealous man, Caroline. A jealous man is a jealous man".

"The trouble with Hugh is he's like an overgrown schoolboy. I don't think he's dangerous, so much as childish and foolish".

She hoped she was right.

CHAPTER 8

It was still quite early after Heather left and Caroline determined it was time to get some answers to a few questions.

For instance, what had Hugh gone to Alex's home for on Sunday morning? What had been said or done which had caused such a violent change in Alex's attitude towards Caroline? Whatever had happened between them had obviously precipitated Hugh's appearance at the Sanctuary and angered him sufficiently to snatch back his word processor.

His vehemence and offensive behaviour towards Caroline was altogether something else. It was a side of Hugh she had never seen nor indeed, relished seeing again. His language towards her had distressed and frightened her.

There was only one way, she decided, and that was to try to get Hugh to admit to what was happening. Being on her own it would be foolhardy to ask him to the Sanctuary. No! Far better to talk to him on neutral grounds, preferably somewhere reasonably public. Surely he would be unlikely to throw a scene in public like the one he had so recently enacted on the driveway? At least anyway should be safer in a more public situation in case he attempted to manhandle her again.

By the time she rang the Broadway Practice,

evening surgery had begun and it was only with great reluctance that the receptionist agreed to get Hugh to the 'phone.

"Now look here, I'm damned busy – who is this?" he demanded angrily.

"Hugh", Caroline said softly, "I'm sorry to…"

"Oh, Cal…it's you", his voice changed instantly, "I thought it was a blasted trade representative who's been after me all day".

Caroline knew he was covering up.

"Hugh, I know it's not the best time, but I didn't realise you'd have begun evening surgery – I ought to have been more aware of the time", she apologised, trying to win him round to an affable frame of mind.

"Cal, for you, anything – how can I help?"
Could this possibly be the same aggressor who had so recently called her a 'bloody little tart'?

"Hugh, can we meet? I've a feeling we need to talk, you and I. You caught me very much by surprise this afternoon. I'd just arrived back from Cornwall".

"Oh?" he sounded surprised.

"I took mother to her sister's for a short holiday. She's been quite dispirited recently and…well, you know, what with losing Dad and…" she felt she was rambling on too much.

"Cal, I didn't realise you'd had a long drive – I'm sorry I got mad, will you forgive me?"
Where did he think she had been? His sudden change of mood was unsettling.

"Can we meet tonight then?" she pleaded.

"Of course, shall I come out to your place?" he offered, a little too readily.
She thought quickly.

"Well, I've a call to make first in your part of the

world anyway, so perhaps I could meet you in Broadway?"

"Okay, he agreed, fancy a drink at the Lygon Arms about eight thirty?"

Trying to sound delighted with the arrangement but inwardly squirming, Caroline said,

"Sounds great – in the lounge, then?"

Although she had a couple of hours to get ready, Caroline quickly showered and slipped on the peach leisure suit which she was well aware advertised her figure adequately and would undoubtedly lead Hugh to think she had made some effort for him.

For more than an hour she hovered about, constantly looking from the window at the front, down the gravel drive and to the main road in the vain hope that Alex would appear. Then she recklessly took her binoculars up to her bedroom which gave out across all the scrub and woodland, expecting she might even see him in that direction. Why should she? She'd told him never to come that way again. And he had respected her wishes. Heather had said nothing about Alex.

She was no further forward now than she had been on Sunday morning. The last three days had been filled with torment. She had spent agonizing hours unable to answer the nagging questions which troubled her. She was in dire misery because she longed to see Alex.

Making the effort and forcing herself to confront Hugh could be dangerous but at least it would fill in the hours of anguish she was going through. She needed to occupy her time and her mind and although there was plenty to do at the Sanctuary, she simply couldn't bear to be there tonight on her own, waiting, praying Alex might turn up.

Imprudent she might be, but at least there could be some answers by the end of the evening. And although outwardly she gave every appearance of self-possession and confidence, inwardly Caroline was timorous and apprehensive. She had noticed the readiness to change his mood in Hugh. Surely he had the astuteness to discern something in her. Earlier this afternoon she had told him she had no intention of marrying him, and now she was playing a softer melody.

Duplicity and guile were definitely not Caroline's trademarks, but she hoped only to find answers – there was no treachery in her or any long-term deceit.

She had always been so ingenuous and uncomplicated.

Unfortunately, she totally distrusted Hugh, had an aversion to him physically and despised him for his unscrupulous behaviour.

The evening did not promise much, but Caroline would use it to her best advantage.

She didn't intend to be late and keep him waiting but that evening Broadway was packed and it had been extremely difficult to find a parking place – even on the Lygon Arms.

Hugh was still in his suit from evening surgery.

"Sorry, Cal, I overran – it's been really hectic tonight. I've not had a chance to go home and change".

Caroline doubted that it would have improved matters from her point of view if he'd been in top hat and tails.

"I must say you look dishy yourself though, Cal", he added, licking his lips lasciviously.

He kissed her on the cheek, more as a formality, Caroline thought, just to show everyone in the Lounge Bar that he was the Possessor. She tried to respond with some kind of warmth but the hypocrisy of it all nauseated her. Over drinks later he took her hand in his.

"I never thought you'd want to see me again after the way I spoke to you this afternoon, Cal. Will you forgive me?" he pleaded, his eyes searching hers. His hand was cold, clammy and uncomfortable but she replied reassuringly,

"We all say some dreadful things when we're worked up. I must admit, though, I've never seen you so angry".

"Believe me, Cal, that wasn't me talking. I've been really up against it these last few days".

"The computer, Hugh, it was cruel of you to snatch it back like that, though. I know it's yours, but … well, you only had to say you needed it back, you know".

"But that's the point, I don't need it…" his voice trailed off.

"Then why? And Heather said you've cancelled your sponsorship on the Newsletter for the Sanctuary…"

Hugh shifted awkwardly in his seat.

"Alright, Cal, you've got to know sooner or later. It's that bloody Sinclair", he said bluntly.

"Sinclair?"

"I've had him up to here", he declared hotly, indicating to the top of his head. "Talk about bloody perverse! Truth is Cal, he's destroyed Julia, you know!"

"What on earth do you mean?" she inquired

gently, hoping to draw Hugh out. Certainly it appeared that when he was angry or roused he could not readily control his tongue.

"He's really led her on!"

"In what way?" Caroline queried, not wishing to sound too pressing.

"Oh you know, she said he's promised her this and that and the other. He's given her to believe they'd marry, of course – it was all just a question of time. But for weeks and weeks he's left her out in the cold. Shunned her. Got somebody else now, by all accounts. Dropped her, easy as that!" he flicked his fingers emphatically.

"How do you know he's got someone else? Perhaps he's just been busy?" She hastily jumped to Alex's defence.

"Come on, Cal, don't be coy. He's been sampling your goods as well, by all accounts!" he added brutally.

Caroline was shocked and it registered so quickly that even Hugh amended swiftly,

"Well, that's what he puts about anyway".

His embarrassment was plain. He had not intended to confront Caroline in this way.

"I don't know who the 'he' is, but their facts are quite wrong, Hugh", she resounded.

"I'm glad of that Cal, and thanks for your honesty", he touched her on the knee.

She squirmed inside her leisure suit.

"Frankly, I wanted to put one on him on Sunday", Hugh continued.

"Hugh, it's none of my business, I know, but what's brought all this on?"

"Let me get you another drink", he responded

somewhat evasively.

She watched him at the counter, jostling for the barman's attention. He was such an insignificant looking man, his crumpled and dishevelled appearance only adding to her revulsion of him. But she had to be very careful not to rankle him. She wanted some information from him.

"So you've taken your mother to Cornwall?" he ventured on return. "I think that's good, she'll probably heal better from her loss away from the Sanctuary".

"My sentiments absolutely", she concurred. "Incidentally, Hugh, talking of the Sanctuary, do you ever see anything of Oliver Cory?"

He flushed noticeably.

His hand was unsteady as he put his glass of beer on the table in front of them.

"Oliver Cory? Good God no! Haven't seen him since … now", he assumed an air of such heavy recall that it was obviously overdone, pursing his lips and shaking his head negatively, "it's got to be since, let me see … no, I tell a lie, I did see him, before the fire, about a week before, actually".

Oh you abject liar, Caroline screamed inwardly. How hard it was, though, to appear casual when she was boiling inside.

"Does he live fairly locally?"

"What's the problem? Actually I've no idea where he comes from". A trace of irritation had crept into his voice. "I hardly know him, in fact".

He continued his line of prevarication.

"Oh, sorry, Hugh, I shouldn't have bothered to ask you – it's just that mother said you'd actually given him a good reference when he…"

"What is this Cal – some sort of bloody persecution?" he fumed, "I told you I scarcely know the chap. You're the second person in a week to ask me about him and I'm damned if I'll be blamed for what happened".

"Really, Hugh, no-one's blaming you", she said, placating him, "I just wondered why he'd never reappeared since the fire".

"So that is it", he grimaced tightly, "you do think Oliver Cory had something to do with it? Oh, oh Caroline – I can read you, young lady, you and Sinclair are a couple of snoopers, but you won't catch me out". He picked his glass up to drink.

She knew she had touched the raw nerve with Hugh.

"Sinclair's got nothing to do with my simple enquiry, Hugh".

"Wrong again! He hasn't primed you too well, has he?"

"I don't know what you mean. Primed me? I haven't seen Sinclair".

That part was true, she admitted. She wanted to see him, yes, desperate to see him, too she was!

"Well you needn't expect to see him at my practice anymore. He's tried to get me to believe he's seen quite a great deal of you, in more ways than one, I suppose".

Caroline was stunned. Surely Sinclair would never have divulged anything to this snake of a man.

"I've sacked him anyway!" Hugh said and she caught the malevolence in his eyes.

"I'm not really interested in what you've done to or with Alexander Sinclair", she lied, praying she was convincing Hugh of the truth in her statement.

Hugh relaxed.

"Really? I thought you and he…"

"Nothing Hugh. You know me surely? I'm a Vet first and last! Chauvinism leaves me cold. At least I've never had to fight for my professional credibility with you!" she added, squirming inside with the total insincerity of her words.

He drew himself up and shifted his seat alongside hers.

"That's one of the most decent things you've said to me for ages. I do respect you as a Vet. I'd respect you more as a woman, too, if only you'd let me get near you sometimes".

Before she could respond to his second-rate flattery his hand was on her knee and he slipped his free arm around her waist, drawing her to him. His beery mouth was on hers before she knew what had happened.

She felt sickened. But the nausea from his fumbling approach was nothing compared to the shattering anguish she experienced seeing Alex appear in the doorway to the Lounge. He saw the situation in a glance. Hugh had his back to the door and was unaware of what Caroline saw over her shoulder. Alex glared straight at her, his eyes burning hatred. He was gone then in an instant.

She wanted to pull herself away and run to Alex across the crowded Lounge, but Hugh gripped her more fiercely around the waist and added insult to injury as he whispered to her,

"You know, I don't want you to take this the wrong way, and I know it's a bit of a cheek, but how would you feel about joining me in the Practice?

There is a vacancy now Sinclair's gone".

"Are you serious?" She was glad to divert him to talking.

"Never been more serious. You'd have to 'chip in' a bit, of course", he added slyly.

She warmed to the situation. "No strings, Hugh?"

"Not yet, I wouldn't want to push you if you are interested. Fancy another drink?"

"Why not, let's be reckless", she started to lead him on, "better make mine a fruit juice again please, I've quite a drive".

"Why not stay up with me – go home early in the morning?" he leaned into her as he got up, his eyes dancing with the possibility.

"It's the Sanctuary, I'm afraid. I've got the keys and the kennel maids are actually waiting up for me", she excused.

"I'll get the drinks", he replied tersely.

Caroline was beginning to think the situation might get out of hand and hoped she could keep her head long enough to get the information she required.

"What made you get rid of Sinclair?" she asked casually as he sat down, hoping he was still in confessional mood.

"For a start, he never played straight. I found out last week that he offered to buy you out! That really got my goat".

Oh, you hypocrite, Hugh Morrison, she agonised.

"No wonder he spent so much time at the place while you were abroad – all the time he planned to sweep the place from under your feet".

"I can't believe it", she lied, "I thought you and Sinclair called there a lot together".

He reddened, bumbling, "Well, I ... to be candid Cal, I did go a lot myself – but my motives were perfectly genuine, I promise you. I, well ... I have to admit that I thought that if I got a bit of a foothold with your old man it might improve my chances with you!"

Caroline winced as he referred to her father in that way.

"But Hugh, my father didn't decide on my relationships", she cautiously reminded him.

"You know what I mean. You've not shown me this much attention since you were at Cambridge. I thought I might lose you. I thought your old man would put a good word in for me. But that bloody Sinclair, he's always insinuating himself and queering my patch. And after the favours I did him getting him into my Practice. Your old man started to favour him, you know. I tried to let him know what a swine Sinclair could be – be he wasn't prepared to listen".

"What did you say to my father?" Caroline egged him on. The three or four pints had loosened his tongue.

"I told him I wanted to marry you, of course. God knows what Sinclair said, putting ideas into your old man's head. He was always there. Cory told me he was there practically every day and a lot of evenings too", he rushed on, incriminating himself at every word with Caroline. "Well, I tell you, it sent our relationship at the Practice absolutely sour. He's been a swine with me for months now".

"But what on earth did he want with the Sanctuary? Hasn't he got acres of his own?" She couldn't let on she'd seen his mini-mansion and practically half a county he owned!

"To stop me getting my hands on it, he said. Oh yes, I told him you'd marry me, then he couldn't have it".

Caroline had heard enough. How she managed to extricate herself from Hugh that evening she never knew. But he was partly drunk anyway and she suggested he sober up a while before driving home.

It was with the greatest relief that she turned the key in the ignition, switched her lights on and drove home.

It had been a close thing, but she had the answers, in part, to what had been going on. Admittedly it was Hugh's version and knowing his inability to tell the truth and his capacity for embellishing fact with fiction, she could imagine the rest.

He had lied about Oliver Cory. There was some kind of chicanery and that would be the next thing to unravel.

She would have to let Alex know what had happened this evening. But that wasn't going to be easy after his entrance into the Lygon Arms tonight. He could never have known what she was doing but would soon understand when she explained.

Just as she signalled to turn into the Sanctuary the powerful headlights of a vehicle reflected in the rear mirror. The car shot past her at great speed and she could have sworn it was a Saab. Was it Alex? She sat in the car on the drive for some minutes, hoping it might come back. She could have been mistaken she told herself, but all the same…perhaps he'd get in touch with her tomorrow…? At least his presence tonight meant that he was back from wherever he'd been.

If only Heather was more forthcoming. She wouldn't jeopardise her relationship with Heather though, just to get to Alex.

The hours dragged interminably at Cheltenham. They weren't terribly busy and it left her too much time to dwell on Alex Sinclair. Twice she picked up the 'phone to Heather to see if there were any messages, but there was nothing.

Alex made no attempt to get in touch with her. Heather mentioned her brother only briefly, saying he'd been like a bear with a sore head that morning. He'd been out quite late the night before and she teased him about nights on the tiles.

"He practically bit my head off", she admitted, "but he'll come round, he's never angry for long".

Heather had not read her brother too well on this occasion, though, for whatever it was eating away at Alex, it was more than another week before Caroline saw him.

Every day was torment to her.

To drag herself to Cheltenham each morning feeling so desolate and filled with aching longing for Alex was the hardest thing she had to do. There was no contacting him. She knew that. Eventually they would meet and Caroline could take her lead from his attitude.

In the first place she was aware from the hate in his eyes that he hadn't expected to see her in Hugh's arms at that moment.

The explaining for that little compromising situation would be a difficult enough task. Harder still it would be to indicate her feelings of need, to arouse him into wanting her and loving her as he had pleaded in the shrubbery.

On the Saturday morning he dropped Heather off because her little old car had to be serviced. He was about to pull away when Caroline ran out to attract his attention.

"Won't you even come in for a coffee?" she pleaded, as he professed to be in a hurry.
Heather came to the rescue.

"What's eatin' you Alex – it's unlike you to turn down a coffee?"

He gave Caroline a disparaging glance but hauled himself unwillingly from the car and agreed to stop. Heather declared she had a lot to get on with in the office and left them alone in the kitchen.

It was still an awkward situation with him. His lips twisted wryly as he looked at her, saying nothing.

"The arrangements are well in hand for the Open Day. I expect Heather's told you", she tried desperately to engage him in conversation.

"I've not talked about your business, Caroline – how you progress now is your own affair", he replied tersely.

"Oh? What's changed? You were pretty keen to involve yourself before?" she persisted.

He gave an exaggerated sigh of intolerance and eyed her cynically, his voice harsh.

"Do you know what kind of game you're playing, Caroline?"

His eyes were hardened as he took the mug of coffee she handed him.

"I can explain about the other night, Alex", she implored him, "I know it looked pretty bad, but …"

He slammed his mug down and reached out,

grabbing her by the wrists, pulling her closely into his body. She offered no resistance, pliant in his grip. She gasped his name as his mouth bore down on hers ruthlessly with a fiery hunger. It was just what she wanted and she yielded into him.

"There's no need to explain anything to me", he rasped harshly, "I know everything", he added confidently.

She felt reassured. His hands slid to her bottom and he pulled her in tightly to his hips. She thrilled to him, her body was aching for his touch. He caressed her mouth with his own and teased open the softness of her lips with his tongue. His tongue then explored the warmth in a rhythmical, sliding motion and she moaned uncontrollably, her breathing short and dry.

"I can make you want me this easily", he whispered hoarsely through her hair as his hands pulled at the front of her cotton blouse, the buttons tearing off as he reached for her breast.

His own breathing was harsh and irregular as his hand caressed her breast, the pink swelling throbbing beneath his touch as his finger and thumb fondled the nipple. He buried his head across her breast and he sucked warmly, drawing her nipple then touching it against the hardness of his tongue. Caroline's body seemed boneless. Her legs were collapsing beneath her as the desire overtook her. Her eyes were shut in ecstasy as his mouth sought hers again.

"Alex!" she squealed, pleasure searing through her.

He was fierce, almost cruel in his possession of her and was fainting with pleasure. He buried his head in her bared shoulder and she felt his lips pressing deeper and deeper into the soft muscle, then his tongue, with its hard, throbbing, pulsing pressure, caressing the skin. Suddenly she felt the sharp edge of his teeth as he ran them across her shoulder, tantalising until the pressure increased and a throb of ecstasy caused her to call his name as his bare teeth bore in more heavily, and she felt the conscious awareness of pain, hard and sweet as the flesh was gently eased between his teeth, rhythmically back and forth along her shoulder. Then his lips, moist and tender, kissed along the bruised muscle.

She moaned with delight, and tears of physical release trickled down her cheeks as the tenseness was taken from her. His arms tightened around her. His mouth touched and brushed hers delicately, teasing, tantalising, scarcely resting for a fraction of a second at each touch, leaving her craving, demanding, aching for pressure. The turbulence within her was bursting.

"Alex, I've missed you so", she cried.

With a sudden shock to her system that left her reeling, he pushed her wildly from him and picked up his coffee.

"I notice just how much you've missed me, Caroline", he thundered harshly. "You've just proved how easily you'll give yourself to any man. And I've seen it for myself, remember?"

Caroline gripped the edge of the cupboard, all colour drained from her face.

"You can't believe that … that … you don't really think that there is anything between me and Hugh …?" she stuttered.

"I believe my own eyes, lady, much as I don't like what they reveal sometimes", he snarled.

"Please, please, Alex …" she began but he cut in ruthlessly.

141

"Don't try to get around me with your cool explanations. You confirmed what I'd suspected. God, Caroline, I wish I'd never bothered to take all the trouble on your behalf. What should I care now who looks after your damned Sanctuary. It's your father's dreams, not yours", he added cruelly.

"Alex, I beg of you, please don't..." she was sobbing, "Alex, you're tearing me apart, please don't..."

"Morrison is welcome to you", he flung at her icily. "I wish I'd not bothered to come looking for you, anyway, you might as well know now why I did – you'll find out soon enough anyway. Oliver Cory has been arrested. You can say what you like to your precious Hugh now – just don't expect any favours from me. You'd have been a bitter disappointment to your father, I know that!" he tossed at her viciously as he strode out of the door.

For long minutes that seemed like hours, Caroline attempted to calm her frayed mind and body. Misery and humiliation swept over her as she sat down on the kitchen chair, unmoving, utterly numb. He had played with her, shown her how easily he could rouse her to do whatever he wanted. She had yielded into him, willingly, wantonly, offering herself, giving herself away to him. Then he had thrown her down. Discarded, unwanted. He had toyed with her body and destroyed her mind

There had been no chance to tell him what she so desperately wanted him to believe over the incident with Hugh. He had closed his mind after making his own judgement.

Her plans and thoughts had gone completely awry and she doubted now if Sinclair would ever believe anything she said again.

More bitter to accept, even than his rejection of her, was the stinging comment he made as he had left. He must have been only too aware of what a cutting thrust it would be. His friendliness with her father surely had revealed how deeply they had loved each other as father and daughter. Her father had been immensely proud too, and Caroline had always known his weakness was his inability to resist talking about her at every opportunity.

No doubt, as the two of them had shared a drink on long winter evenings, as her mother had since led her to believe, then Caroline's name and praises had illustrated a paternal affection that was overwhelming to an outsider. Now it ripped at her emotions more fiercely than ever. It was bad enough to be reminded of how she had always only tried to please William Franklin, but worse than anything was the harsh reminder that her father was no longer at hand, no longer able to protect her as she learned to cope with situations that had no answer in textbooks.

One moment Alex Sinclair had raised her emotion to fever pitch, disturbing sensations that had always been dormant. He had effortlessly drawn from her passion that had been waiting to flower. Innocently, guilelessly, she had capitulated under his skilfully persuasive, intimate technique and exposed herself with all the vulnerability that her inexperience could produce.

Then, with flagrant disregard for her sensitivities, he had cruelly pushed her aside and thrust a knife into her. Now she bled inwardly in a fever of agitated emotion.

How could anyone human being be so ardently

passionate one minute only to become so glacial, cold-blooded and antagonistic in the next instant? Even animals did not behave in sur irreconcilably, contradictory ways, she conceded. If he was able to 'turn on' his passion at will, like going to the tap for water, then how could such actions be trusted? Surely it proved that his feelings were feigned? He could blow hot and cold whenever he felt like it without any consideration for another's sensitivities.

Unaccustomed to such fickle behaviour, Caroline was totally helpless as to how to cope. She was not by nature someone of racy, unpredictable manners, and to come face to face with the mercurial temperament of Alex Sinclair destroyed her self-confidence.

How naïve she felt. How utterly degraded and ill-used. Her disillusionment was total as she shifted herself helplessly through the day, doing her utmost to avoid Heather's anxiously inquisitive eyes.

Imprudent she might have been, she conceded, silly and trusting even, but disingenuous – never! And Caroline vowed nothing and no-one would mesmerize her again in the way that Alex had, using his beguiling attraction to sway her from rational thought. She was only thankful now that her mother was in Cornwall, for she would have been unable to avoid her maternal perception.

The last thing Caroline wanted was to burden anyone else with her emotional problems. Spending so much time alone through childhood and adolescence had equipped her with an indomitable strength to 'keep herself to herself'. She had always made her own decisions, been her own counsellor and she would not change such ingrained traits now.

No doubt she could talk to Heather. After all, his sister probably understood him better than anyone else. She could confide in her, very probably, even ask her to intercede on her behalf with Alex.

Pride, however, would restrain her. Not only that, Caroline allowed herself, if he needed persuading of her feelings by a third party – if he couldn't accept her at face value – then he was certainly not worth bothering with.

Someone ought to be in a position to rationalise for themselves, she conceded.

CHAPTER 9

For days after Alex's brutal words to her, it had been like walking in a long, dark tunnel. At night there was little sleep, only the restless, feverish nightmares of loneliness that come from the realisation of loss, despite all her resolutions and clear rational thinking. Emotion and logic she had realised, were two incompatibles and there were many moments of weakness when all she had decided about shutting him out of her life meant absolutely nothing. Thoughts and actions were also two incompatibles!

She cried until exhaustion took over somewhere in the early hours before dawn. The devastation of her situation did not seem to abate and each morning the disillusionment of the day had to be faced. Her chance of seeing Alex was zero. He had purposefully avoided her now for nearly a month.

It was the lowest month of her life. Each day she dragged herself to Cheltenham to Avery Briggs' cheerfulness and good humour that scarcely lifted her spirits, no matter what. The only thing that drove her was the years of discipline and forcing her mind to accept that her life must go on without Sinclair. The pain was not assuaged but she knew all the clichés about 'healing Time' and eventually he would cease to be important to her and the ache would go.

Caroline had never let any man touch her or reach her in the way Alex had. He had demonstrated only too clearly that he was master of a physical control over her. Her body had been brought alive by his touch, her senses had been exploded. And even though there had been no fulfilment, the promise had been there, the inducement to further intimacy that would lead to the consummation of her emotional and physical needs.

And now it was all gone. The hope, the promise, the opportunity to experience love. The desire he had had for her was obviously gone. It was all dead and she could no longer dream of what might be in store for her. He had made it palpably clear that he was disgusted with her, that he regretted his ministrations towards her. Caroline's ordeals would cease to be his responsibility, if indeed they had ever been in the first place.

Deep down she knew she would always grieve for what might have been with Alex. He was too deeply in her mind to be dismissed. He lived too close for her to ever have peace of mind again.

The Sanctuary Open Day was her only salvation. Despite Heather's hard work, there was still much to absorb her attention and although her mind was only ever half on the job, at least it occupied her and helped her to pull herself back to some kind of normality.

A week before the function, Heather arranged for local newspaper coverage and Caroline was forced into reviving some of her old 'joie de vivre' for the eager interviewer.

"Is it true you've worked with Rhinos?" the young man asked, "it could give us an interesting angle for the introduction".

She didn't see the relevance but it amused the interviewer.

"How do you feel you are coping after the problems created by the unfortunate death of your father?" he threw at her.

"I think he'd be proud of the success now", she responded swiftly, slightly shocked by such a tasteless question, "as a matter of fact the manageress of the Sanctuary deserves all the credit".

Heather blushed in the background, shook her head and wagged her finger at Caroline in mock anger.

"She's the sister of Alexander Sinclair", Caroline added, "he's a local Vet who was so helpful to me personally. He was a close friend of my father. Without him, I'm sure we'd not have survived".

Her voice was positive and filled with praise for Alex, but her heart was forlorn.

The interviewer picked up the strains immediately and tried to infer something of a possible romance for the future?

Caroline was quick to denial. Too quick perhaps for the astute, young male interviewer who persisted in raking about for more information of Alex Sinclair.

"Was he a friend from University, some Vet school, perhaps?"

When he had exhausted that topic he pressed her for stories of her background, university days, childhood and so on.

"Why did you want to become a Vet in the first place?" he prompted.

"Look", Caroline fumed, beginning to lose her patience. "I thought that this was to be publicity for the Open Day, not a potted biography of Caroline

Franklin".

The young man and his photographer smiled. They knew how to make a story interesting and startling, and on this occasion they certainly did!

"What the hell do you mean raking about in my private life?" Alex demanded, flinging the local newspaper down in front of her two days before the Open Day.

"I didn't write the article", she declared defensively, stunned at his angry mood.

"Read it!" he commented threateningly. "How dare you involve me!"

She stood for anxious minutes, her heart pounding as the words jumped out from the headline.

SANCTUARY FOR LOVE

Caroline Franklin, whose solicitude with the Rhinos of Africa, found solace of her own in the protection of her near-neighbour Alexander Sinclair. "Without him, I'm sure we'd not have survived", Caroline told our reporter, Michael Stoneway. The Sanctuary holds an Open Day on this coming Saturday and clearly Mr Sinclair and his sister, Heather, have taken the tough little lady of Rhino fame under their wing!"

Caroline couldn't read on. A tear trickled slowly down her cheek. There would be no sanctuary for her love. She looked at him despairingly.

"Do you deny you said all that?" he growled, his hands on his hips, his mouth twisted sardonically. There was contempt in his face.

"I never said all that about ... you must believe me", she pleaded helplessly.

"Don't give me that rubbish! Publicity like that is nauseous. I can do without that kind of shallow praise. Whatever I did was for your father", he flung angrily at her. "God knows what he'd say to this…this tawdry kind of third-rate rag publicity…" he shouted, pointing at the article furiously.

"Ask Heather, she was here", was all Caroline could say, "they twisted my words".

"For God's sake, Caroline, I've a profession to uphold, a face to show round the County. What are people to think of me when they see this?"

"I can only say I'm sorry", she sobbed, holding the edge of the chair for support. "Heather arranged to get us some publicity for Open Day on Saturday – I had no idea it would lead to this kind of thing. In any case," she stirred into anger, "it's equally as offensive to me, don't you think? I haven't asked for my name to be linked in that way. You're not the only one likely to be put out by it, you know!"

There was a peculiar tenseness between them as their eyes met fleetingly. She had been forced into an angry defence lest she break down. It was her only way to combat her need for him. Clearly his mood towards her was not changed. With a shrug of his shoulders he made to leave, and she called him back.

"Alex, will you, will you…are you coming on Saturday?"

His eyes swept over her with an insolence.

"That's a bit of a damned cheek after that blasted article!" he snapped, a sigh of intolerance in his voice.

"I never wrote the article, Alex".

He paused at the door, his eyes resting on her, almost reluctant to leave her.

Dryly, in desperation, she pleaded, "Please Alex,

I beg you, for…for my father's sake, if nothing else".

There was a catch in her voice as she added, "Mother has decided to stay away – she can't bear to be here and I … oh, Alex," she began to feel tears welling, "I'd be grateful to have the support of a man on Saturday, please…"

"Ask Hugh Morrison, he told me he's to be your protector", he tossed at her cruelly and, as he turned on his heel he inflicted one more caustic and stabbing blow. "For a woman who declares herself against chauvinism, I consider that request a damned nerve!" Caroline fled to her room and threw herself on the bed, and let the tears come.

The rejection, the cruelty of his remarks had been a sharp thrust to her. Even in his parting moments when she had tried to win him round she had crawled and begged for some comforting crumb from him. No pride left in her, all the anguish and humiliation wracked her body. She felt crushed as she buried her face in the pillow, sobbing deep painful sobs that shook her whole body.

She felt that Alex had changed her, awakened her then shattered her innocence. Nothing would ever be the same again. It was a long time before the tears subsided and she fell asleep with sheer exhaustion. Avery Briggs came to the rescue, volunteering to help her on the Saturday. It relieved her considerably to know he would be around.

He had been to the Sanctuary on a number of occasions and met Heather. In fact, it had been the one bright spot in her last few miserable weeks when she had introduced them, for she had never been more pleased to see two people come together so easily.

"Och, Sinclair never told me he was hiding you at home when we met in Edinburgh", he had grinned, taking both her hands warmly in his. They had hit it off so well and Caroline was well aware that they had been seeing quite a lot of each other since that first memorable meeting.

He came around after his evening meal on the Friday night to go over last arrangements for Saturday.

So many tickets had been sold and they were expecting hundreds of visitors. The local radio station had offered to loan a public address system. Through the generosity of the local TV Birmingham they had arranged to provide a celebrity guest from the studios to officially open the function. The tickets which had been sold had already covered the cost of all the expenses and so Heather was clucking excitedly at the prospect of raising plenty of extra funds.

In terms of things to see at the Sanctuary, there was very little that would sustain interest for long, despite the extensive kennels, new cattery, bird house and rabbits and so on. Heather's plan had been to have lots of interesting and exciting events taking place to keep the visitors stimulated and engrossed. All the events would be free, naturally. Raffles, pony rides, competitions and stalls would be the main 'money-spinners'.

"Of course", Heather added, grinning, "the refreshments will be very popular – funny how people can't get by without lots of tea, squash and biscuits". The Women's Institute had volunteered to furnish them with home-made cakes and local ice-cream sellers had volunteered to have the vans available on site all day on a percentage sales basis. It was surprising what kind of interesting events Heather had scavenged for, including a display of falconry. There was a dog training and obedience session being put on twice throughout the afternoon by a group from Evesham. Significantly, the dogs would all be mongrels, many of which had actually come from the Franklin Sanctuary, according to Heather.

Weather permitting, it promised to be a really exciting day, starting with a parade from the village to the Sanctuary by the local brass band who had agreed to give a rousing start to the proceedings. Piped music would be played then throughout the afternoon.

Caroline only wished she could feel less melancholy. Her mother had been in touch by 'phone many times during the month, but didn't want to come back to the Sanctuary until after Open Day, if at all. It was nothing to do with anyone or anything except her inability to see the Sanctuary in the same light anymore.

When her husband was alive, it was almost like a 'retirement venture'. Caroline could see now, in retrospect, that that is just what it had been and just exactly what her parents had wanted. It was something to potter along with, kept them busy and satisfied. Her father's dream had been one of contentment, restful, steady, day-to-day coping. Now this was all something different. There was an urgency about everything.

Regretfully, Caroline admitted to herself that Sinclair had been right – it was her father's dream – not hers anymore.

Right now she didn't have a dream that she could

hang her hopes on. She was so downcast on the Friday evening after Heather and Avery Briggs had left.

Her thoughts were filled with the idea of selling up after all and going away.

Clearly, with her mother's interest waning fast, she wouldn't want to be trying to cope alone. There was no saying just how long Heather would stay on anyway. And Caroline didn't want to stay around making a fool of herself, longing for a man who had made it blatantly clear that he had no interest in her now. Had he ever had, in fact? Perhaps she had deluded herself into thinking that Alex's displays of desire and physical craving had been something more than they really were. After all, it was maybe a passion of the passing moment, a transitory feeling of lust.

It didn't help matters for Caroline to recall that she had tried to avoid him from the first time she had encountered him at Ledbury during her training days. Since then all manner of emotion had passed over her, filling her at times with confusion as she tried to come to terms with what had really happened to her.

They say love and hate have a thin line dividing them – the two most powerfully passionate of our emotions. Caroline had crossed the line, willingly or otherwise, and had now only love for the man she had first hated. Everything he had said had ceased to matter and now she wanted him more than anything else. She had got her priorities into perspective at last, but it was too late! He had shunned her abominably and crushed her into a state of abject humiliation and misery.

It continually brought her back to the one resolve of selling up. Naturally, her mother's agreement must be sought, but under the circumstances that would probably not be too difficult since her mother had already declared an interest in staying with her sister.

How to handle the situation would be something she must discuss with Mr Devine.

He was no longer a 'little man of dread' whom she didn't relish meeting. Since the upsurge of the Sanctuary's finances and well-being, he had made a few visits and frequently given his quiet reassurance and satisfaction about the way the venture was progressing. She was sure he would give sound advice and might even handle the whole wretched business for her to avoid some of the inevitable heartache she would probably have to endure.

He could even know of a likely purchaser – perhaps Sinclair might still want to take it on! That would be a bitter irony, but one she was prepared to accept. It would all be expediency in the final analysis. Rather Sinclair than Morrison, at any rate!

Selling would be difficult enough but deciding what to do with herself would present an even greater problem. She had a job, of course, but could she really stay so close to a man like Alex? Always there would be the factor of 'what might have been', and strong though she knew she would have to be, she knew her mental strength did have its natural limits. So near and yet so far, to waste away emotionally, longing for what was lost or might have been.

Short of making herself into a complete fool she would do virtually anything, but humiliation at Sinclair's hand would be unthinkable.

It occurred to her that there was a wealth of opportunity still abroad – so many rewarding ventures she could become involved in. Finance was not the issue really, for there must be something to come from the land sale which she would be entitled to under the terms of her father's Will. She would immerse herself in her work once more. After all, it had been a tonic before, so why not in the future? Her professional Veterinary magazine was constantly advertising enticing overseas posts. Her mind began to settle on the idea as she tossed and turned through the early morning hours.

Animals don't kick back, she reminded herself, and remember flashes of some of her overseas experiences, forcing her mind to concentrate on thoughts other than Alexander Sinclair.

Dawn was almost breaking as she finally fell asleep to snatch a few hours before the long day ahead. At least Heather's superb organising had everything so much under control that Caroline's role for the whole of the Open Day was only nominal.

"You must just play Lady of the Manor, please Cal", Heather had urged, "the work is for us to attend to – you need to be on hand for everything, but do nothing!"

"But I must have something to do, surely there's a job written into the day's programme for me, Heather?" she asked, knowing only too well that time on her hands was the last thing she wanted.

"Avery and I will keep control for you – have no fear", she assured.

Caroline had smiled inwardly at the way Heather had recently been linking her name with her brother's friend. She had been so wrapped up in her own wretched unhappiness, that she had scarcely noticed the love blooming between the two most unlikely people. And yet it shouldn't have been a surprise for they were two hardworking, self-effacing, gentle, caring people - and they were both lonely. Avery Briggs was a very understanding and warm man, as Caroline had quickly realised. He had no illusions about himself but he had a nature that would endear him to someone like Heather. All the time she had been at the Sanctuary, she had only once mentioned the loss of her soldier husband to Caroline, and she must have found such a contrasting welcome relief in the character of Avery Briggs who laughingly declared the only battle he ever had to fight was with his weight! So little was said but so much understood between the two of them.

Sadly, for Caroline, their manifest joy was a constant reminder of what she might have been experiencing but for her own foolhardiness. She cursed herself for trying to take on Hugh Morrison that night in the Lygon Arms. Duplicity had never been her line of country and she ought to have had more sense to think she could outwit such deviousness. Worse, she ought to have confided her thoughts in Alex. How different it all might have been!

From the very beginning the Open Day was a hugely successful venture.

All day she had thrown herself into the activities, going the rounds, being seen by her volunteers, shaking hands, smiling until her face ached, bearing up under all the warmth and well-wishing.

And all day she had constantly scanned the crowds for the face of Alex, which had never appeared. It shattered the last remaining shreds of illusion in her to think that he would not even put in an appearance – if not for her sake, but that of his sister, whose dedication had brought about the Open Day in the first place. Caroline had been tempted more than once to ask Heather if he would be coming, but her better judgement prevailed. In the last weeks, Heather had said nothing but there was something implicit in her unvoiced, quiet sympathy and Caroline was grateful that explanations were unnecessary. Her crestfallen, dejected manner had not gone unnoticed and yet Heather had sensibly not got herself involved in her brother's affairs.

Late in the afternoon, Caroline sat in the Marquee to drink a cup of tea, and despite all the hustle and bustle going on around her, in spite of all the crowds enjoying themselves, she felt desolate and lonely.

"All on your own, Cal, on such a momentous day", Hugh Morrison's voice piped in on her thoughts and he edged himself down at the tiny wooden table. "Can I join the hostess?"

He was the last person she had been thinking of, or wanted, but it was a relief to have someone to talk to, even though she considered it indelicate of him to have turned up at all in view of the circumstances. How could he have known that Alex would not be here, for he might have presumed so, if he had read the recent local 'rag'.

Everyone had been passing her with short, polite conversations all day and she could rely on Hugh to be blunt, down-to-earth and indecorous.

"What a surprise", she commented.

"You thought I wouldn't come, I suppose", he said sulkily, his face pouting peevishly. He took her hand clumsily and added, "Cal, all things aside that have happened in recent months, I do think a hell of a lot of you, you know!"

His attempted honesty was disarming to her but she tried to respond.

"Why Hugh, that is kind – I'm glad you've come – it's been such a … such a wonderful day", she finished, hurriedly, a choke coming into her voice.

He responded immediately.

"Here", he said, jumping up, "let me get you out of here, Cal, you could do with fresh air, it's all a bit much for you, I reckon".

He slipped his arms around her in a brotherly fashion and without a demur she allowed herself to be led from the Marquee, across the lawn and towards the open fields.

"You spend far too much time on your own, you know!"

She began to interrupt him.

"No, let me go on … I know you think I've been a cad, maybe I have, yes. I've connived to get you – what chap wouldn't? I admit I've tried to…well, I've…I've always thought you and I would be … you know…" he trailed off.

The mere thought nauseated her, but she let him have his rein as they stopped by the field gate.

"Things haven't gone too well between us since … since, well, since your father's … since your father died. That's probably my fault as much as anything, Cal. I've been jealous – it's Sinclair, always with his quiet, insinuating ways, he completely undermined my confidence about you".

She cast a quick glance at him. He was staring back up to the centre of activity around the marquees and the stalls. His face was taut and his eyes distant, as if his thoughts and words were being conjured up so far away. Nothing he said had any meaning or relevance because she found him so disgusting now, trying to excuse his loathsome behaviour and his lies.

"Confidence in me for what, Hugh?" she asked simply, turning abruptly from his arm clasp and leaning against the gate.

"Surely you've always known I've wanted you to be my wife?" his face looked so stupid to her because the whole idea was so preposterous, she almost exploded half with anger, half with hilarity at such a fatuous, asinine possibility.

"Do you have any idea what I've schemed to keep you?" he let his stupid thoughts ramble on.

"Keep me? Keep me, Hugh?" she finally exploded, turning on him suddenly.

"Well, you know what I mean", he started.

"You have never even had a foot at the starting line. I'm sorry to have to disillusion you, but I've never wanted to be your wife".

"It's that bloody Sinclair again, isn't it?" he said menacingly, "he's queered my pitch ever since I let him into the Practice. Bloody foreigner!"

He gripped the rails of the gate furiously, blood rising in his face, a nerve twitching at his temple, as he continued vehemently, "Let me tell you, Miss High and Mighty Franklin…"

"No", she burst in on him sharply. "And you'd better calm down, Hugh, before you let any more cats out of the bag in your temper!"

"And what do you mean by that, may I ask?" he spluttered, reddening even more.

Caroline took a deep breath and a big chance. It seemed minutes before she answered, but in the mere seconds that elapsed, she gained confidence to make her accusation.

"Oliver Cory!" she announced firmly and turned her body and face full at him to confront what he had to offer in reply.

He stared at her, fury in his eyes, but he was unable to think quickly enough.

"You ought to have known better, Hugh, than to consort with common criminals. Arsonists always burn the match too closely in the end. You are aware, I'm sure, that he's been arrested – so you'd better be careful now, because you could find that once he's in a jam, he might loosen his tongue and your duplicity will be exposed".

She knew she was guessing, but did Hugh?

He made a start to walk away.

"I seem to have hit your raw nerve, Hugh".

"You bitch, you bloody little bitch…all this time…" he spluttered.

"Get out of my sight – the further the better – in fact I shouldn't wonder the police aren't already looking for you", she added, shocking him further.

"Why, you…you bitch – you and bloody Sinclair…"

"How do you think I could marry a man whose evil machinations killed my father?" she thrust at him as he took a step towards her then thought better of it.

She had put two and two together and got four. He stomped furiously away, not daring to open his mouth in reply or turn to look at her again.

"You murdered my father, you paid someone to burn his Sanctuary and you destroyed his life", she screamed after him, oblivious to everything else.

"You've lied and cheated and indirectly you've murdered my father… I'll make sure you…that you never…never…" she was still shrieking after him, whether he could hear or not, and she broke into paroxysms of sobbing and fled through the gate towards the woods.

Somehow, Whistler found her and caught up with her and hours later, it seemed, she calmed down enough to walk back, empty but dignified, into the waning moments of her Open Day.

When everyone had left she sat down for a celebration drink with Heather and Avery Briggs and told them both what had happened with Hugh. Her explosive accusation had not exactly been a cathartic experience but she somehow felt more in control now the fact had been exposed to him.

It occurred to Heather's common-sense mind and Avery agreed that Caroline could herself be in danger from Hugh.

"He's got a lot at stake, Caroline", Avery tried to make her see sense. "We'd better stay on tonight and make sure you're all right, then in the morning you must make a statement to the Police".

Caroline was too numb to resist their protestations and gladly acquiesced, but not before telling them she proposed selling up.

They were both stunned.

"Och, you're just down with the whole onerous business", Avery assured her, his arms around her comfortingly.

"No, truly, it will be for the best in the long term, this is not a quick or momentary, rash decision. I've had it in mind since…since mother went away to be truthful". Knowing she wasn't being entirely truthful because she couldn't be, under the circumstances, she continued, "She won't come back. I spoke to her earlier today, and I'm sure she'll be glad to leave it all behind. It's not what it was, you see…"

"But Cal, that's my fault, I've just taken possession without realising", Heather interpolated with sincerity.

"No, Heather, you've made it what it ought to be. But it's not what mother and father had in mind. Somewhere quiet to end their retirement days, just being happy together, toddling through, just making ends meet, caring for…looking after the unwanted – that was their dream".

Heather coloured uncomfortably.

"I'm sorry, Cal, I…"

"Don't be", Caroline interrupted her, "it's how it ought to be now. Without Dad, my mother's dream died. It could never have been anything to her without him. And in any case, who knows how long they would have been able to carry it on in their own happy, carefree way. They would probably have got into an intolerable financial mess, and that would have been far worse for them to endure. It's much more practical the way you've been managing it, believe me", she reassured her.

"But you can carry it on Cal, surely", Avery said familiarly.

"No, not alone I can't".

"But selling? What will… what will I do now? Where can I go now? I love it here, Cal", Heather asked anxiously.

"Then have it, Heather, with my blessing", Caroline suggested.

Avery Briggs looked at Alex's sister and no words needed to pass between them.

Their mutual agreement was implicit in that look.

"Terms, Cal, terms?" he asked.

"We'll agree on that I'm sure", Caroline responded, relieved. "But there is just one condition which I must ask for the moment", she confronted them both.

"Just the one?" Heather laughed.

"Yes! Whatever else has to be arranged and agreed, I must ask you to promise to say nothing to your brother Alex".

Heather's face was suddenly serious and she knew better than to argue.

"I understand fully, Cal. You have my promise", and she moved across to hug her friend with a deep understanding. She had watched Caroline suffering for weeks and had said nothing. Much as she felt close to her, she respected her Veterinary friend's privacy too much to encroach with advice or caution or indeed anything.

She did not need to be a psychologist to read her friend's melancholy and yet, knowing her brother was behind much of Caroline's trauma, she could and would not interfere. Her loyalties to her brother were equally as strong as to Caroline and she had long since vowed to let nature take its course. Many times she had longed to reassure her, but knew she had no right. Her brother was blinded by his own pride. 'What will be, will be', was Heather's philosophy.

Avery Briggs had asked Caroline to take time out to think again about her decision, but her mind was made up. When the necessary details had been gone through with Mr Devine she started to feel some relief that some of the burden of responsibility of ownership had already left her.

She began to look seriously for another post, although Avery had offered to transfer the practice in Cheltenham to her as part of the price towards the Sanctuary. He intended to give it up now, he had confessed, and settle into a more dignified, leisurely existence with Heather at the Sanctuary.

Caroline wrote after more than half a dozen overseas posts which took her fancy and agreed to take a holiday while waiting to hear from them.

It cheered her considerably to hear that Hugh Morrison had been arrested a week later and, according to the local reporter, Hugh had some considerable questions to answer for in fraud at his Broadway Practice, let alone his duplicity in the now indisputable arson attack on the Franklin Sanctuary earlier in the year. According to the scurrilous Michael Stoneway, reporter, 'new and interesting evidence had been brought to light and two men would be appearing in court'.

"He'll be in for a long spell at Her Majesty's pleasure, I guarantee", Avery had announced the day the news broke out.

Caroline felt it was only just desserts and had no sympathy to express for Hugh.

It confirmed all she had ever believed about him anyway. She wondered what would happen to the Broadway Practice, but reckoned it was none of her business anyway.

She had made a decision to take herself down to Cornwall for a few days and she would stand by that plan, despite the desperate urge to see Alex Sinclair. But even as she pulled out of the driveway into the lane, she involuntarily stopped longer to look to the right, in the vain hope that he might be coming in her direction.

Out of sight, out of mind, she thought as she pulled up to cross at the next junction.

She wondered if she was doing the right thing. Alex had once made an offer for the Sanctuary and in letting it go to his sister and Avery Briggs, she had excluded his option entirely. Still, if Hugh did serve at Her Majesty's pleasure as Avery had suggested would happen, then perhaps Alex would pick up the threads at the Broadway Practice. He'd have plenty to occupy himself then, and would have no need for the Sanctuary.

Early autumn sun was flickering through the trees as she drove out of the County, her mind in torment. Cutting Alex out of her life was a necessity if she was to survive. If he had still wanted the Sanctuary he would have appeared at the Open Day, she reasoned.

He had taken little or no interest in its affairs since the day after they'd been for dinner at Cleeve Court. That must be a strong indication of his disinterest. Still, perhaps she ought to have given him the option...

CHAPTER 10

Another week had gone by.

Caroline decided to tell her mother what she planned to do.

There was a chill sea breeze as they walked along the sands, Whistler deeply engrossed in burying herself in a hole of her own making. It had been a very relaxing week, not without sadness for Caroline, but not wishing to spoil other people's pleasure, she had tried to forebear with their kindness and gentle questioning.

Her mother always knew when to back off usually, but it was she who raised the future of the Sanctuary.

"Didn't you even ask Alex?" her mother eyed her curiously, not wishing to accuse or blame.

"He hasn't been around for weeks", she replied.

Her hands dug deeply into her jacket pockets, her fists clenched to quell the real emotion that was welling up inside her.

Looking out to sea, her voice quaking but distant, in concert with her thoughts, she added, "I'm going abroad, mother".

They walked on in silence for a couple of hundred yards before her mother slipped her arm through her daughter's.

"I've never interfered in your life, Cal. You've always been your father's girl – strong-minded, self-willed, self-possessed – but now I'm not so sure I can't ... I have to say what I must, dear".

Caroline waited. If she had tried to speak she would have betrayed her pent-up feelings to her mother.

"It's Alex, I know".

"No, mum, he's ... well, that's only a small part of it", she lied.

How could she bring herself to tell her mother the whole sordid story?

"You were his condition, you know – didn't you realise? He and your father had it all worked out. Still, that's another of life's plans gone wrong. Best to say no more about it".

The silence was killing Caroline.

"Do you mean that I was a pre-condition to his purchase of the Sanctuary? I don't believe it. How could anyone bargain with my life like that? What right had he and father?" she asked angrily.

"It wasn't quite like that, Cal. Alex loved you. But you were so opposed to him for so long…" she trailed off.

Caroline couldn't believe it.

"He insulted me…" she ranted.

"That was when you were a student – he told us all about that", her mother smiled confidently, knowingly.

"You knew?"

Caroline's exasperation was unbelievable. Whistler ran to her side as she shrieked out in utter disbelief.

"Your father was ... he looked forward to… oh, Cal, so much ... he was so proud of you. And Alex.

He put you on a pedestal and said, 'one day she'll climb down to me, Bill'. And now you've … it's all … Cal, let's go back now. All these plans people make … we should just let life come to us, instead of racing out thinking we can be so instrumental in altering the course of things. Let's walk back now, Cal. I'm a little tired, dear", she said with an air of finality.

Nothing more was said between them and Caroline choked inwardly, wishing things could have been different. The pattern of her life had been set by parents who cared too much for her ever to 'talk' to her. If only they had shared more of their thoughts and conversation.

Why, oh why, she screamed inwardly, was it always too late? Why don't people talk to each other? So much had been left unsaid, so much damage done by their decency and gentle rectitude.

Her aunt Olivia, who had a good idea what was going on, quietly suggested to Caroline that she leave her mother behind and go back to 'sort things out'.

"It's a bit late for that, Aunt Olivia", she responded sadly.

"Of course it's not child – learn from the folly of the older generation – go and find him – talk to him".

"I tried that, really", she hesitated, remembering the embarrassing scene in the kitchen that Saturday morning, and then later his harsh words when she'd pleaded with him to come to the Open Day.

The vehemence in his voice and the look of insolence he had given her as he flung the wounding retort about Hugh Morrison had left a strong impression on her mind.

"I'll say this, Cal, pride is a very high price to pay for anything in life. I won't forget Jacob Trengrouse who works for me – the day he came to my door, pride all gone, nothing but his bare hands to offer. Just to survive he offered the last thing he'd got, and he came to my door. God be thanked I knew and honest man when he needed me".

She stomped off into the kitchen, her homily to her niece over.

Coming home had not been so easy, but Caroline had taken the advice of her elders and determined to 'give it one last chance'. If Alex still spurned her then she'd take her other alternative and go abroad for a while.

Some replies had come into the posts she'd written after and interviews had been offered the following week. Caroline found out from Heather that Alex had been away but had no idea when he would return. It was a daily wait for Caroline to see if he returned and each day that passed her confidence evaporated a little more.

Mr Devine had been dealing with the transfer of the Sanctuary to Avery Heathcote Briggs and it made it so much easier for her that decisions had been made and acted upon so readily. But her own plans to confront Alex appeared to have completely misfired. She had hoped to see him before going to London for her job interviews, but that was not to be, and another long weekend elapsed while she contemplated afresh the wisdom of her actions. As she left on the Monday to go to the two interviews she felt as if Fate had conspired against her once again where Alex was concerned.

She took all her credentials with her and during the two days of interviewing she was offered both posts, each wishing her to take up employment as soon as possible. Going overseas again would answer so many of her problems, and she drove back from London having promised to provide her interviewers with an answer within two or three days.

Feeling particularly confident, probably due to her recent success in London, she drove straight to Cleeve Court and her heart raced as she pulled up behind Alex's Saab.

As she pulled the ancient doorbell though, the fight went from her and she timorously hoped Mrs B would answer to give her time to gain equilibrium once inside.

"Well?" Alex demanded.

Tall, imposing, dark and angry, he leaned against the door pillar and raked her from head to toe, his eyes resting wickedly on hers as she attempted to sound confident.

"I've come to explain…"

"There's nothing left to explain … is there?" she rasped, forcing her eyes to meet his.

Her heart sank. She had warned her aunt Olivia that he was not an easy man to break through to in this kind of mood.

She was dumbstruck for the right thing to say before he slammed the door in her face as he looked so threateningly about to do.

"Alex, I … I've … please, give me a fair chance", she stammered, fighting back tears that stung her eyes.

"You'd better come in", he volunteered with reluctance and she followed him across the hall.

He arrogantly pointed for her to go into the Drawing Room, but he remained at the entrance to the room, leaning against the doorway. He folded his arms in an aggressive posture, waiting for her to continue.

She looked about her helplessly and swallowed hard, her heart thudding against her ribs.

"Well, he demanded for the second time.

His eyes moved over her and she lifted her chin almost defiantly to stop herself remembering the last time he had stood in the doorway like that, when she had been clad in a silky, black dress.

"I've sold the Sanctuary…"

"Tell me something I don't know", he interrupted her, his voice flat.

"You know? But Heather promised…"

"Mr Devine is an old friend", he pronounced, a quick smirk tilting his mouth.

She flushed.

"But that's professional etiquette – he shouldn't have divulged private information", Caroline said stiffly.

"To hell with etiquette – and where have you been, if I may be so bold as to ask?"

He gave her a steady look and shifted his position to the other leg peevishly.

The silence in the room was crippling as she tried to speak, but no words came. He mesmerised her – she was afraid to come out with anything, playing for a little time, hoping his anger was beginning to subside.

He undid the top button of his shirt, pulled at the tie around his neck and seemed to relax a little.

"You're lucky to find me – I've only just got back from Edinburgh", he flung his tie onto the seat near the door.

She took advantage of the trace of friendliness in his voice.

"That makes two of us", she attempted lightly. "I'm just on my way back from London. I thought I'd see if you were home before I went to the Sanctuary".

"Desperate are you?" he sneered a little.

"Yes!" She replied bluntly, taking him a little off balance.

"Candour indeed", he smirked, his eyebrows raised in surprise.

"I've come down from the pedestal, Alex, that's all", she said slowly, fighting back tears and an urge to throw herself in his arms.

And the statement slowly dawned on him as his body relaxed a little.

"Your mother's been talking to you", he averred, his tongue running sensuously along his bottom lip.

"It's about time someone did, don't you think?" she asked quietly.

"You'd better sit down – I'll fix you a drink", he offered without question.

She sank into the deep leather armchair and let out a huge sigh as he disappeared from the room.

Exhausted emotionally, she was sitting with her head in her hands when he returned a couple of minutes later with a Martini and ice for her, a large brandy for himself.

He stretched himself out in the window seat, his legs extending in a loose sprawling fashion as he eyed her closely.

"Are you in love with Hugh Morrison?" he demanded sharply.

"He's responsible for the death of my father…"

she blurted out.

"I know that", he said flatly, running his hand through his hair, "but that was not the question I asked, Caroline".

She drew in a quick breath.

"How can you possibly think I have ever had feelings for Hugh? What kind of woman have you thought I am? Perhaps it would be better if you didn't answer that", she added, watching the sardonic pursing of his lips.

"You played some very funny scenes, Caroline".

"If you are talking about the night in the Lygon Arms, I can tell you that your judgement of the scene is, without question, totally wrong. I did try to explain to you but when you gave me…"

"If you had viewed the event from where I was standing, you might, too, have put your own complexion on things. Besides, I've had Hugh telling me almost daily that you and he were about to march up the aisle".

She sighed with exasperation and frustration. "Hugh fantasised".

"So did I, Caroline, so did I", he admitted wearily, sighing heavily. is grey eyes looked heavy with remorse and he continued, "You were a kid when I first met you, it seems so long ago. I didn't know Bill then. I'd just joined Morrison – at a price! And what a price! He talked about you even then, how he'd marry you and have a free partner in his blasted practice. Then I came into this", he gestured expensively with his arm. "Cleeve Court". I was in the money all right, with grand ideas to set up in opposition to Morrison to show people what a damned lousy Vet he is, more than anything".

"What stopped you?" she whispered.

His eyes fixed onto her for a long moment.

"I met your mother and father. My new neighbours taught me humility", he said simply, getting up and walking out of the room with his already drained glass.

He came back with the brandy bottle which he offered to her but she declined. He poured a large measure into his own glass and stood, legs astride, staring through the bay window. He flexed his muscles in his tight buttocks, his long legs deceptively sexy sending her frantic by their sensual stance.

"I let him down, your father. I knew something of the little rat Cory – I'd got more than suspicions. And Hugh was ripping off your father blind, charging him for weekly visits".

"Did you ever speak to him about it?" she asked naturally.

"God, speak to him, I never even found out for a long time", he angrily responded. "Hugh was up to no good with his finances for a long time – why do you think I disappeared from view for some time?"

"I had no idea. I…I naturally, I…presumed…" she stuttered with embarrassment.

"Back in Edinburgh they've turned his history upside down because I asked them to. That's where I first met him – same Vet school, although I presume you already know that. Oh no, Caroline, Hugh's chicanery extends further back than you think and goes beyond mere fraud of his own business activities, even, as I'm sure you know, to his payment to Oliver Cory to do away with your father's cattery. I've turned up all sorts of 'dirt' on our loveable Hugh, believe me".

Caroline was stunned. It horrified her to hear the reality of his wickedness and have another person actually admit to Hugh's involvement in the crime against the Sanctuary.

"Maybe I'm being naïve", she broke in, "but why didn't my father stop him coming on these highly expensive visits?"

"He did, eventually, when I moved into Cleeve Court. But, you see, he… I'm sorry to say, your father had no business sense, Caroline. He hadn't really known what Hugh was up to. In fact I only found out because the girl in the office – you know, the one who married and left the County".
Caroline nodded agreement.

"She was a friend of mine, actually, and…" she wondered if she should tell Alex about the price of his partnership, but he must have read her thoughts.

"I think I know what you're going to say – she said she'd told you that much, at least but hadn't the courage to tell you about the charges he was making to your father. She left me to do something about that!" he added ruefully.

"I went to meet him that night at the Lygon Arms…" she began.

"I don't think anything more need be said on that score, I'm sure your intentions were, well, misguided, but well-meant".

"I want to tell you", she insisted. "Hugh has always lied to me, about so many things. I'd seen him giving Cory money, or so I thought it was, and yet he denied ever knowing the man practically. But when he's drunk a little beer, he loosens his tongue and gets carried away. But it…it wasn't until,… on the day of the Open Day…he…" she screwed up her face with disgust at the memory of what had happened by the field gate. "Ugh!" she shuddered, "it leaves me cold and clammy to even think about it. Anyway, I told him I knew everything – and although I was only guessing at much of it, he gave himself away and I knew then that I was right. I saw the police next day, Avery advised it, of course".

"So it was you who precipitated his final arrest?" he asked, amazed.

"What's so surprising about that? If it hadn't been me, Cory must sure have wanted to drag him down with him".

He contemplated her for a long time and then forced her eyes to meet his.

"I then put you on a pedestal, Caroline. I felt you'd grow up one day and then… 'Little Miss High and Mighty', Hugh used to call you – but I said nothing. You had good reason to be up there too! You're a very fine Vet", he admitted, softening.

"Alex, why did you always insult me so?" she asked, a sob rising in her throat.

"No Cal, I never did after Ledbury, now did I? Think carefully. After the way you were at Jordan's farm, when, yes", he admitted, "I was peeved – you had picked up on a fault of mine. I should have been more careful looking at his herd. I took it out on you".

She coloured at the memory of his hostility on that occasion.

"Why didn't you say all this then?" she pleaded. He sat heavily in the window seat.

"How could I? You went abroad. I found out later that you were Bill's daughter – and if you remember on the odd occasions we met you played me wickedly – hardly civil as I recall".

"Can you blame me?"

"In retrospect, I suppose not – but I did try to make amends. From your father I found out more about you than you knew yourself. He worshipped you, so much". He took a careful sip from his glass, watching her intently and then added in quiet measured tone, "I came to do the same. He read all your letters out to me on those evenings we spent together. I knew everything about you. More than anything I could understand how he loved you".

Caroline knew she wouldn't be able to stop the tears from forming on her lashes, nor stem the flow of hurt at the memory of her father, as she listened to Alex.

"I began to wonder if you were mortal. And then Morrison…by God!" The Oath spat from him. "He gave me so many disconcerting tales I could never make out the truth".

She put down her glass and sighed.

"He was odious. The scheming things he must have got up to defy belief. I wanted to tell you the night you took me to Stratford, but I still felt…"

"You didn't trust me, did you?" he asked sharply. She confessed openly. "Not all the time. But after coming to Cleeve Court…" she stopped. This is what you've really come to tell him, she told herself. But still she hesitated, not knowing whether he was ready to hear her raw admission of her need.

"I've never … no-one has…" she was embarrassed almost to admit her lack of experience. "You showed me … what … made me feel, I've never had such intense feelings, not ever … I didn't even trust what kind of feelings they were", she faltered again, tears trickling down her cheeks helplessly. "I didn't know, Alex ... nothing like that had ever happened to me before ... and, and ... I think I began to ... to love you, Alex", she confessed haltingly. "I didn't know if it was love ... or ... I had no-one to ask, I ... I've never talked to anyone before about ... I wanted you to...to show me, to love me, to have me and please", she began to cry uncontrollably and held out her hands to him, appealing.

He was at her side, pulling her close into him, his hands firmly pressing her against him as he pulled her up into his body.

"My poor darling, Caroline". He murmured into her hair huskily.

"Alex, I've been so wretched without you. I've longed for you to come and...I never knew such feelings before...I..."

"And I thought you...well, what fools we've been. Can you forgive me my darling? I behaved so jealously. I was consumed. I saw the best part of my future disappear".

She looked up at him, her whispered breath was hesitant.

"Why did you make me a condition of the purchase of the Sanctuary? You didn't even know me?" she begged.

He smiled.

"It wasn't quite like that, Cal. Believe me. And you're wrong, I did know you. Oh, I admit I couldn't be a hundred percent sure that you would love me, but I suppose I was confident I could make you, win you round with love, care and...well..." he admitted arrogantly.

"But if the fire hadn't...I was going back to

179

Africa, you know…" she reminded him.

"What a tiny word is "if', and with so much potential", he grinned. If I could only start this scene over again, Caroline. If I could erase so much of the unnecessary hurt I've caused. If, if only I can convince you that I watched the Sanctuary night after night to trap Cory and Hugh Morrison – and I did!"

"You did?" she asked, surprised. "But you never said so!"

"No! It would have been imprudent at the time. But I made sure you were safe". He kissed her softly and brushed his mouth across her eyes to assuage her tears.

"Alex, why didn't you come to the Open Day?" I begged you…and you were so wounding and hateful with your reproaches".

He held her from him, his hands gently cradling hers and he said softly,

"Do you think such feelings of desire and need were only felt by you? Caroline, look at me", he forced her eyes to meet his. "I had never experienced such a need for another person. And, I suppose, like any man, when I have as much as half a hint that someone else might also taste such favours, jealousy takes over. There is no other excuse. It's an age-old passion and we rise up in defence", he groaned, pulling her into him once more. "You must believe that I love you", he moaned, finding her mouth with his and bringing his lips down with gentle pressure.

Caroline's body sank into his with a willingness that answered his unspoken question, and she responded to his kisses with passion.

"Today", he murmured huskily, "today, Caroline, we'll start afresh. I love you and I need to feel you close to me, you will never need to ask me to love you, for I won't be able to help myself or stop myself from giving you whatever you need".

"Oh, Alex", she moaned, tears of need and passion mingling as they rolled down her cheeks, "I'm so happy…"

"But why the tears, my darling?" he gently wiped his hand across her cheeks and brushed his mouth across the dampness.

"But I…I…sold the Sanctuary…" she sobbed apologetically.

He pushed her from him to arms-length and began to laugh.

"Oh my dear girl, is that what's upsetting you now. But don't you realise that the original condition with your father was that if I wanted you, I had to take on the Sanctuary as well!" He pulled her into his arms again, only more fiercely. "Think of all the money I've saved!" he joked to lighten her mood.

"You mean…you mean you're not angry about it?" she asked shyly.

"Angry? Caroline, my darling, I'm not angry, I'm delighted with what you decided to do. Heather is over the moon! And old Briggs – he's like a cat with two tails!"

She smiled warmly. "They seem so pleased and Heather has far more idea of how to manage such a venture than I ever could", she said generously. "And Avery has a new lease of life, don't you think?"

"And so will you have, my love. We've a Practice to run in Broadway".

"But Hugh…?"

Hugh has already had the matter taken out of his hands. But we will be changing the name, though. I was up in Edinburgh all last week with my solicitors getting things sorted out. But this is better than I even hoped for, because I didn't know then that I'd acquire a sleeping partner, in the best possible sense, of course", he joked.

"Oh Alex, what a stupid fool I've been. I tried to rationalise so much and ended up going around in circles. I couldn't believe that there was no answer to love".

"Of course there is, my darling", he reassured her, cradling her in his arms and leading her up the stairway. "I think that we should find the answer together, right now, don't you?"

Caroline's response was lost as his mouth came down on hers once more.

THE END

NOTE FROM THE AUTHOR

I love hearing from readers!

You can contact me on facebook
www.facebook.com/karen.passey or by email
k_passey@outlook.com

And if you've enjoyed *Sanctuary For Love*, please
leave a review, so other readers will know!

Printed in Great Britain
by Amazon